CODENAME DUSTOFF

BARREN HILL
BOOK 2

WILLOW SANDERS

Edited by BRIGGS CONSULTING, LLC

Proofread by CRYSTAL CLEAR AUTHOR SERVICES

Cover Design COVER ME DARLING

TRIGGER WARNING

Military Trauma, PTSD, Amputee / IED, brief mentions of
the Afghanistan war

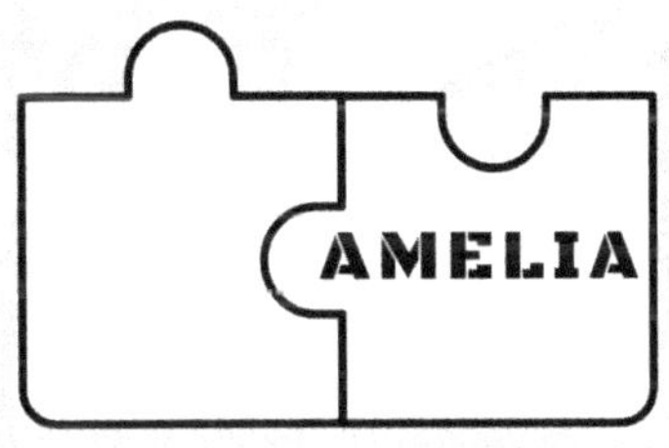

My coming home didn't look the same as everyone else's. For those who returned after serving a tour it was warm hugs, shrieks of joy, crying families with homemade signs, and lots of discussions surrounding the first thing they wanted to do now that they were "home." They were welcomed with the pomp and circumstance which was the expected fanfare. Especially when families have been pining for service-members and worrying about them since the day they stepped foot onto that C-17.

Mine, however, had no warm hugs. Unless you count my family hugging one another in worry. The shrieks—if there were any—would have been in response to the phone call that I'd been airlifted out of FOB Shank, and it was questionable whether I'd survive the transport. The only fanfare greeting me in Germany, I would assume, were the nurses and doctors on standby ready to rush in and stabilize me once I arrived with the rest of the DOs. Dust Offs. That's what they called us. The lucky ones who danced with the IEDs and lived to tell the tale. We got to keep our tags around our necks. We'd see our families again. Even if we were half the people we were when we'd left.

I'd taken a ride on the air cavalry over three years ago. Yet, it still felt like yesterday. Every time I closed my eyes, I could still see my friend's faces, hear our stupid banter about getting back to base because Garcia got a care package from home. His wife and their church family always sent us the best shit. That box specially had been packed with Little Debbie Christmas Trees and every flavor imaginable of Crystal Light. It was truly like Christmas. Even if it was still six weeks away. We'd been anxious to partake in Garcia's wealth after our afternoon AOR patrol. I replayed that scene in my head numerous times a day. It was the Groundhog Day-esque dream that greeted me every night when I closed my eyes.

My *Recovery Care Coordinator*, we called it an RCC, was responsible for my *triad of care*. She was not satisfied with how I continued to miss benchmarks dealing with psychological recovery and connectedness to my recovery unit—called a Soldier Recovery Unit or SRU. Benchmarks were king in the Army. There was always something you had to be achieving. Whether it was a new designation or rank, or your mental or psychological aptitude.

I met with Pam, my RCC, once a month to discuss these benchmarks. Usually, the meetings were pretty predictable. They went something like this: "Hey, you're still below standard for your psychological benchmarks." I would give her some kind of smart assed reply that would suggest losing all of my friends when our Humvee hit an IED may have something to do with that. The look on her face when I arrived told me this visit would not go like other meetings previous.

She tended to wear her glasses on her head when we chatted and didn't put them on until she needed to look at paperwork. But when I arrived at her door, they were already on her face, staring into my file. I was greeted with a terse, "Amelia, right on time. Have a seat."

Her whole office had been decked with Christmas cheer. Something about that grated me. I didn't know if it was the obnoxious magenta Christmas tree or the twinkle lights that framed a pitiful window overlooking a parking lot and train tracks beyond. It felt off. Like she tried too hard to force a cheerful appearance when the whole building was a black hole of depression and despair.

"Your benchmarks dip lower each time I see you, Amelia." She held up a hand to stop me from saying anything before I'd even opened my mouth. "I don't want a maudlin comment about your friends. That is exactly why I'm concerned."

Pam had really curly, jet-black hair that hung in wild ringlets just below her eyebrows. Some days the curls were defined as if she'd taken special care to style them, and other days, like today, they stuck every which way as if she'd been running her hands through them frequently, like she was at that very moment.

"I don't know how else to get through to you, Amelia. I've tried the soft approaches, hoping you'd come to the realization that going this alone won't work. I think it's time for tough love.

Suicide rates among vets are at an all-time high. These test scores." She held up my benchmarks, which showed a steep decline with every monthly check-in. "They're beginning to head into a territory where I would have the authority to remand you into a mental health facility. I promise, you don't want that."

Damn right, I didn't want that. Similarly, I didn't want her in my business. To be frank, I didn't want any of them in my business.

"Don't you think I've done enough for the Army?" I asked, feeling guilty the second it came out of my mouth. "I think that I should be able to figure out how to cope on my own. I don't need Uncle Sam trying to control how quickly I am able to deal with anything in my life."

I point to my useless leg. I was in near constant pain, even this many years later. I wished the doctors would have told me what the rest of my life would look like as they were ordering me to keep breathing, to hold on, that I was minutes away from the hospital.

"Amelia." She took her glasses off and set them down next to her computer. "No one is trying to control the speed of your recovery. We're all here—I'm here—to be the stopgap to prevent you from spiraling down to a place where no one can reach you, and you believe there's only one way out. I convinced your SRU to give you eight weeks."

She handed me a folded piece of paper with the name and address of a resort in a tiny mountain town called Barren Hill.

"There is an amputee support group there. It's the only one I could find within ninety minutes of your house. I'm sorry it isn't geared specifically toward vets."

I folded the paper and put it in my jeans pocket. She could pound sand if she thought I was going to sit around talking about my feelings every week. I would figure this out on my own. Stop at the library or something and get some self-help shit.

"This isn't an option, Amelia. You have to check in and have an assignment slip submitted for each of the eight sessions. They must be concurrent. You may not miss a session unless you clear it with me first. And I'm telling you, if you plan to call me because you don't want to go, it better be for a damn good reason, or I'll ask my friends in MP to pay you a visit and escort you to Thornhill Psych. If you aren't going to fight for yourself Amelia, I'm going to fight for you."

***

"You must be Amelia!" A woman in a chef's jacket scurried towards me. Hearing my given name used by strangers still felt foreign. Even after all this time. It was probably for the best though. Sanchez was attached to too many memories I was desperate to forget.

"Welcome! I'm Gemini Tate." She extended her hand and shook mine with the enthusiasm of a Disney cast member. "There is coffee over there on the table, lunch is buffet style just inside the door, and there's water and iced tea on each table. Here's your nametag—they require everyone to wear them."

She continued to fuss, handing me various pamphlets along with a folder and badge. "We're excited to have another member. This is a small group. Mammoth Slope and Barren Hill are truly underserved by the greater community so any time we can get a fresh face attending, we roll out the welcome mat!"

Gemini Tate appeared to have all of her limbs. Maybe though, she had a prosthetic under her pants. I guess I shouldn't judge. She could easily have moved into acceptance and was living her life to her fullest.

"We heard from the V.A. they were sending someone our way. I still can't believe this is the closest amputee acceptance group in the greater tri state area. It's just a travesty that our veterans are not treated better. Especially after all you've done. Or seen. Or god, all you've sacrificed."

"Are you the one that signs off on my attendance forms?"

I didn't need to talk to anyone about sacrifice. Or what I'd seen. Especially not to some cracked out cruise director desperate to dial up my level of engagement to full blast.

"Me? Oh, no. You'll need to see Henry or Elyse inside, they're both wearing yellow lanyards." She held up her hands with an uncomfortable chuckle. "No. I'm just... Well, you see —" She appeared lost for an explanation, though it was surprising to me she wouldn't have whatever her sales pitch was at the ready for the newcomers. "I'm simply the one who saw a need and had the means to fix it."

I nodded and flipped through the kumbaya bullshit she'd handed me.

"You can go inside." She finally released me from the responsibility of chit chat. "They're probably getting started."

Gemini the Cruise Director hadn't been kidding when she said it was a small group. With me, there were six. All of whom were deeply immersed in conversations when I walked in.

"Amelia? Nice to meet you." The man saluted me first, then shook my hand. Just what I needed was to be singled out from the onset. Aside from the fact that I wasn't an officer, and presently wore jeans and a T-shirt, and not anything that would identify me as a former member of the military. "I'm Henry Jennings, this is my co-leader, Elyse. We're so glad to have you here. You can take a seat at either of the tables, but we'd love for you to introduce yourself to the group first if you don't mind."

Of course, I'd have to stand in front of the "class" and give my spiel.

"Name's Sanchez. Um, Amelia Sanchez. I've been an amp for going on three years. This was the closest support group to me."

"Well." Henry rocked back and forth from heel to toe, waiting seemingly for me to say more. There wasn't anything else I cared to share. "How about we go around the room and you all can introduce yourselves to Amelia?"

Eight weeks. That was how long I'd been told I needed to attend. Honestly, latrine duty at Shank seemed like the better option.

With the exception of the seasons, not much changes in Barren Hill. The same people who lived here when I was a kid, still do. Most of them live in the same houses, or on the same plot of land. We all shop at the local Pack n' Sack, get our cars serviced by Jared and his pop, Larry Flynn. Flynn was their last name. I don't know why everyone called him Larry Flynn as if we were in Georgia and that was his first and middle name. That's just how we did it up here, I guess.

If you weren't a mining family, you were a rail family. That is, of course, unless you lived in the Abilene portion of Barren Hill. That's where the fancy gated community folk hailed from growing up. The ones whose parents were suit and tie people that drove fancy cars to whatever job they had. Abilene was the place you rode your second hand bike past on your way to school and imagined being one of those kids. Their Christmases surely were a parade of new suits and dresses, patent leather shoes and fur lined jackets, and oversized boxes wrapped up in gorgeous gold and silver wrapping paper containing video game systems or Cabbage Patch dolls.

Me and my pop were rail folk. He was a foreman for the rail yard and as soon as I graduated high school, he lined me up to start my career path at the good old BNSF. Finn's dad owned the town's watering hole, so like the rest of us, he too was born into his role. College? No one talked to any of us about that. When I lost my arm, I just had to deal because that's what we did up here. We dealt with the hands we were given. We figured it out. Adapted. Found ways to continue spinning on the hamster wheel.

"Emmett, can you help me...please...I ...it's just barely...out of...maybe if I stand on my tippy toes..." Gemini stretched her fingers as high as her arm would allow it to extend, attempting to hang yet another piece of garland. It looked as if I'd stepped into a Christmas movie set. Every wall, fixture, booth, and tabletop at the Tuckaway Tavern was adorned in some kind of holly or jolly. In all the years prior to Gemini buying into our bar, The Old Lady, as she'd formerly been known, we'd never displayed much Christmas cheer. I guess revamping and rebranding also meant taking a more active approach in the holiday season too.

"Given your propensity for tripping, sliding, slipping, or

falling, how about you let someone who doesn't need a step ladder hang that."

Gemini huffed in my direction, never taking her eyes off of me as I hung her decorations and adjusted the ribbons.

"Tell me again why we're doing all of this?"

"Because it's the holidays?" She went back to rummaging through all the shopping bags she'd brought, in search of some glitter covered who knows what to accompany all of the greenery.

"I asked the same questions." Finn walked up beside me, wiping his hands on a dish towel. "And also told her that hill folk don't much care about all of this—stuff." He waved his hand in the general direction of Gemini's shopping bags.

The MetroCenter was over an hour away. I don't know if I ever cared enough about Christmas to drive in the snow to the mall to get a bunch of shit that would be out for a month collecting dust and chucked back into plastic bins and stored in the attic for eleven more months. It seemed pretty pointless to me.

"I swear I'm going to call the two of you Ebenezer and Scrooge!" She pointed a green and red plaid bow in my direction, the glitter that tinged its edges showering the table and floor.

Finn wrapped his arms around her, cradling her from the back.

"Nothing Scrooge-like about either of us, Princess." He kissed the back of her neck, resting his chin in the dip of her shoulder. "We just know this town. This ain't suburbia. People here kinda stick to themselves."

"You're both wrong and I'll prove it."

The fight drained out of her, and the comment was more a sigh than an actual statement. Usually, their in-your-face burn for each other chemistry didn't bother me. It actually made me really fucking happy Finn finally found someone so perfect. Sometimes though, watching the two of them hurt like hell.

"I'd love to tell you both to get a room, but Jasper is gonna be here any minute to talk to us about Gem's new bourbon experience."

I'm sure it was because Christmas was just around the corner. The whole holiday was one gigantic billboard that reminded lonely people like me just how much their lives sucked in comparison to the Rockwell-like existence of everyone else. Like all those TV commercials where the wife with perfect teeth and a cashmere sweater wakes up looking like a fresh-faced Disney princess and skips outside to a snowy landscape to find a new status symbol parked in her driveway. Or even the simpler ones where the huge family comes pushing through the entrance to their mom's house, weighed down by packages and pies, and they all gather around a gigantic table and break bread. Every day during the holiday season, consumerism told us what happiness was supposed to look like.

My holidays growing up consisted of my dad taking both the morning and afternoon shift at the rail yard because they paid double time and a half. Working on Christmas day meant we could dig ourselves out from the credit extended to us at the Pack 'n Sack, or any of the other stores in Barren Hill. Christmas dinner was cold cults and milk if we were lucky, between my and Pa's shifts. Finn and I would hang out together at the bar, which was where his pop spent his holidays. Sometimes, if we were lucky, the patrons of The Old Lady would give us each a dollar or two as a "tip."

"Bourbon experience? What the—who's gonna show for this?"

Finn turned the pamphlet from Jasper over in his hand. I'd been so deep in my trip down memory lane that I hadn't realized Jasper and his associate Harmony arrived.

"Jasper is a private label distiller. His bourbon, *Lakshmi,* is highly sought after, Finn." Gemini smiled at our guests, explaining the purpose of the meeting to Finn. "Jasper is a friend of mine. I met him at Chef Tobin's restaurant; he was Tobin's exclusive distributor.

"Given the holiday season is so popular up at Echo Creek, I thought this would be a great local experience that gets them into The Tavern. We're in hill country, bourbon and whiskey are practically synonymous with this region. What's more local and touristy than a bourbon or whiskey tasting?"

I thought it was brilliant. Especially given the clientele up at the resort. Finn didn't appear convinced.

"In addition to our *Lakshmi* private selection, my friend Harmony has created a new app to enhance the tasting experience."

Harmony launched into an explanation of how the data obtained from the app could help inform future purchasing decisions for the bar. It could be set up to ask questions about specific types of bourbon, or spirits in general. Finn at least seemed to perk up when she mentioned geo fencing and pushing advertisements to customers that are within a few hours driving distance of the Tavern.

"This is going to be great!" Gemini's smile stretched across her whole face. When she got jazzed over things having to do with the restaurant, it was impossible to not get excited right alongside her. Given she was a classically trained chef, it was evident she knew her stuff and had a finely honed instinct for what would work and succeed. However, as her friend, and knowing all she'd walked away from to move here to be with Finn and help run our business? I just loved seeing her excited. Witnessing her enthusiasm, for me, showed me over and again how much we needed her without ever knowing. Plus, it couldn't be overstated how perfect the two of them were together.

"I am so glad that the two of you were able to pay us a visit." Gemini stood and pulled Jasper into a hug sometime later. "But I have to leave you in the capable hands of my partners as I'm needed up at the resort."

As soon as she said the word hands, Jasper and his friend looked right at me, their eyes wide with mortification. It sometimes charmed me how afraid people were of offending me. But days like today, when I already had a burr in my britches, their discomfort is what grated me.

I didn't need to be up at the resort for another thirty minutes. Usually, I didn't like to be the first person there, because it made me look desperate. I also didn't want to sit around the tavern and have Jasper and Harmony stare at me like a zoo animal with manufactured sympathy in their eyes.

"I'll come with you, Gem! I think I remember Elyse saying she was going to be late today."

Despite only having one arm, I was out of my chair, wrapped in my coat, and falling into step next to her with the speed and efficiency of a bobsledder.

"You never volunteer to come early, and given Elyse texted me twenty minutes ago telling me she was on her way, I know you're full of shit. So what gives?" Gemini looped her arm through mine as we walked the path to the resort.

"I hate when people stare." I waived my armless shoulder as an exclamation point to my statement. "And that stupid look they get when they notice I only have one arm."

"I'm so glad our amputee support group is helping you to accept and release."

That was one of Henry's favorite mantras. Accept that we were different and release ourselves from personal expectations. At least three times a meeting, he would tell the group based on whomever was sharing an experience, "I see that someone is reeling in what they just cast out to the universe." Or he'd say, "Expectations are not fish. We do not want to pull them back in. Release them! Like butterflies!" It was a thousand percent hokey, but still managed to dill my pickle every time he said it.

Over the summer, we'd hosted a wedding for friends of the resort owner. In a moment of weakness, I'd broken open like a fucking egg to Gemini. Watching all the blissfully happy couples dancing, laughing, and socializing with one another, had been too much to bear. I told her things Finn didn't even know. That I was afraid I'd be alone forever. I didn't think anyone would ever want to date me. Who would find a guy who wasn't capable of holding hands and opening a door concurrently, attractive? And my ever present fear of my inability to open a pickle jar. In every area that counted, I came up lacking. With me, the partnership would be inequitable from the onset.

Gemini tried to get me to attend a support group for months but realized amputees weren't at the top of the list for any kind of funding in these parts. Money was tight and no one wanted to waste it on people with missing limbs. Especially not when women up in hill country were still dying in childbirth because they didn't have access to healthcare.

Instead, she called Penn, who owned the Echo Creek Resort. One request to underwrite her new venture, and now we had a support group. There were five of us in the group up until a few weeks ago. That's when Gem was contacted by the Veteran's Administration and asked if her group accepted veterans.

"Oh, hey! Amelia! It's so great to see you again."

Speaking of our new friend, she arrived early. Both times I'd seen her, she wore her hair tied in the tightest bun I'd ever seen. Based on the bumps along the hairline, it appeared her hair was fairly curly. You'd never know though, considering every piece of hair, even the flyaways were contained beneath bobby pins and probably hair products.

The woman was definitely equal parts enticing and surprising. Last week she stood in the corner of the room, leaning against a support beam, for the whole meeting. She barely participated, other than providing her name. She was a TFA, according to Gem. A transfemoral amputation, with a side of disarticulation. I'd only learned that listening to Henry and Gemini's conversation while they reset the ballroom. I didn't know her story. Given she was a vet, my guess was that she'd lost her leg overseas, Afghanistan or Iraq.

Amelia nodded at Gemini, giving her a barely heard "ma'am."

"I'm so glad that you came back. It's truly a great bunch here. I know being new is always hard." Gemini reached for her hand and squeezed it, that genuine smile of hers glittering like a damn Christmas tree. "If you need anything. Seriously, anything, please let me know. I feel kind of responsible for everyone who attends this group. In a weird way, it's like I'm connected to all of you."

Henry called to her from inside of the ballroom, asking about chairs.

"I'll be back in a few minutes. There's plenty of time before the group starts. They're setting up all the holiday decorations around the resort for the tree lighting tomorrow—you should go check them out! With the snow outside and all the lights—it's just magical!"

Chit chat and small talk were not my forte. Actually, I pretty much sucked at striking up random conversations with people. Most of my interactions with strangers were in the form of online friendships and the occasional dating app. At least then, the angle of the camera could hide what was obvious in person. There was no use pretending my existence didn't make people really fucking uncomfortable.

"She's actually a famous chef." I tossed my head in Gemini's direction. "She came here last year and fell—literally and figuratively—in love with my best friend while staying at the resort. Moved here to be with him, and now they're happy as all get out."

I don't know what possessed me to lead with a story about Gem. My communication skills didn't get near enough practice in this town. Amelia didn't appear all that interested in what I had to say anyway. She leaned against the windowsill, her eyes dancing all over the space, looking everywhere but at me. I wouldn't be surprised if I made her uncomfortable too.

While I continued to flounder like a damn fish gasping for air to revive this stilted conversation, her cell phone rang. She raised her eyebrow in tandem with bringing the phone to her ear. Like I gave a damn about her conversation. I turned away, but it was a small area, and her voice carried.

"No sir, of course, I do. I appreciate the invite. I just don't think I'll be able to come. It's not about the money, sir. With all respect, those men don't want to see me. I'm just a reminder of all the bad shit that happened over there. Yes, sir. I understand. I will think about it."

They disconnected. I heard Amelia slump into a chair, whispering a string of expletives. I should have kept to my business. Finn always says I'm nosier than an old widow on her front porch in summer.

"You okay?" I asked, taking the seat opposite her. "You're not in any pain, are you? It sounded like you came down pretty hard in that chair."

Wrong approach. If she'd been fixin' for a fight when she hung up, I'd dialed her to thermonuclear. Even under her zip hoodie and stretch pants, she looked kind of buff. She could break me in two with minimal effort.

"I'm sorry, who are you?" she asked.

Her whole face was flushed, from her ears all the way down to her chest. I didn't want to assume she was on the verge of tears, but the deep chocolate of her eyes glistened from light streaming in from the window.

"Emmett McCarthy." I extended my hand. "Fellow amputee. Also, generally a nice guy who is concerned for your well-being."

She ignored my extended hand, choosing instead to open her text messages on her phone and shoot off a message to someone.

"I have some Aleve in my backpack if you'd like it. Sometimes the cold makes this ache too."

I raised my shoulder realizing too late I was in a sweater, and she couldn't see what remained of my left arm. The gold medal for conversations that aren't awkward at all should be awarded to me.

"I'm fine."

Her gritted teeth said otherwise.

"I couldn't help overhear." I pointed towards the alcove where she'd taken her phone call a moment earlier. "I can certainly empathize if you want to talk about it."

"You can empathize?" she asked, with a snotty cock of her eyebrow. "So you served as well?"

This was probably the reason that I didn't initiate conversation with people I didn't know. I always ended up sticking a foot in my mouth. Only two weeks into meeting this woman and she'd probably already put me on the *never in a million years would I date you* list.

"Not with that. But I've been on the receiving end of people feeling uncomfortable around me. Especially people I used to work with who would rather not look at me or be around me anymore, because I remind them of how dangerous working on a rail yard can be."

"I'm *fine*," she repeated, this time with more emphasis. I desperately searched for a way to pivot the conversation but couldn't think of anything. For the first time in years, I had that first tingle of a connection, and I was one pitch away from striking out.

"Hey, you two, the meeting is about to start!" Gemini called from the ballroom.

At least I was saved from further making myself look more awkward than I already did.

CHAPTER THREE

I swear the entire earth conspired against me these days. First this forced daisy chain self-love fest I had to attend every Saturday. This was number two of my eight-week sentence in purgatory for not getting better fast enough. What irony. When you're in the Army, you're taught to take your fear, your anxiety, any normal and rational feeling you have and compartmentalize it. You're supposed to shove it down to a place where it won't become a distraction. Then you get home, and all those feelings you've been burying for years begin to surface. When their tests say you aren't dealing with it properly, they say, "Shame on you soldier! Why haven't you learned how to cope yet?" All the while forgetting we've been conditioned to refute asking for help at the risk of appearing weak.

I'd joined the Army as a means to escape all of this claustrophobic existence. To go and be something other than married at sixteen with a brood of kids, who struggled every month to try to feed everyone on miner's wages. Yet here I was. Living at my parents' house in Haven's Cove, existing with the whole damn family again.

It figured that none of the towns around here had any access to good doctors or support programs. And naturally the closest V.A. was over three hours away. It was crap that Pam and my former C.O. conspired to make these visits part of my required regiment of care. He'd just called to "check in," because as a friend, he was worried about me. What did he know about lost limbs? He still had all of his. And three tours of duty complete, a wedding to look forward to at the end of the month and a cushy fucking desk job waiting for him whenever he was ready to take it. That wedding. He'd mentioned on his call that I hadn't RSVP'd. While he didn't speak the words, he sounded hurt. Which was a punch in the fucking gut. I hadn't been part of his unit long enough for me to bond with the team like the rest of them. I'd barely been two months into my tour of duty when we'd hit that IED. Yet, he treated me as if I'd been under his command as long as the rest of the group. Even while still dealing with a mess in Afghanistan, he would check in with my doctors in Germany to get regular status updates.

I owed him the respect of attending his wedding. The guilt ate away at me. There were so many reasons why I didn't want to go. I could probably fill a whole notebook. When he'd offered to pay for my plane ticket just so I could go, I'd nearly drown in my own shame. I would never be anyone's charity case. That just wasn't happening. If I had to drive two days and sleep in my car to save some money I would before accepting a handout.

But that wasn't why I refused. I didn't want to be a distraction from his big day. And when a woman with one leg comes walking into a wedding—people will stare, and not in a "where did she get her dress, it's so beautiful," kind of way.

"It's pretty, isn't it? With the snow coming down? As much as I hate the actual holidays, I'm a sucker for the whole winter wonderland thing."

The guy with one arm—he'd introduced himself as Emmett—continued to linger despite the call to join the group. That smile. Jesus. He had a smile that could charm the skin off an alligator. It was all soft pliable lips, a hint of teeth, the barest lift of his eyebrow. I bet he got a lot of phone numbers with a smile like that.

"Unfortunately for me, all of that white stuff means slick sidewalks and roads, hidden tripping hazards, and as it begins to melt, ice. I honestly wish I could be as taken by the quiet magic like everyone else, but I've landed on my ass far too many times to count and trying to get back up is a bitch."

Disarming. That's what his whole sweet-lipped charm was. Who was he to me? Nobody. Just someone else who drew the short stick in the poor unfortunate souls lottery. He just wanted to make idle chit chat while we waited for our meeting, and I'd managed to take a grenade to his enjoyment of the season.

"It's a shame actually. How an injury can suddenly make you hate things you used to love."

He nodded, resting his head against the fogging glass. While he didn't say anything, I could see a shadow in his eyes that told me he understood what I said. Maybe that look is what prompted me to be so revelatory.

"Haven's Cove has a pond in the town center. As kids we'd check every day for the town council to raise the green 'safe to skate' flag. My sisters and brothers and I would pride ourselves on being the first ones out on that stupid pond."

Funny how many things that used to be things I loved, now were things I loathed. As kids my two siblings closest to me in age and I would play synchronized skater on that pond. We would spend hours practicing made up routines, preparing for pretend competitions.

"We're about to get started, you two!"

Gemini called us into the meeting again just then, thankfully saving me from this unnecessary trip down memory lane.

"I'M PRETTY SURE the hotel is solid."

Emmett approached me where I stood off to the side of the room.

"The people who own the hotel," he continued, pointing towards his friend giving me that soft lipped smile I'd admired earlier. "Gemini, over there, is a friend of their family. Rich east coasters. Old money types. Anyhow, that doesn't matter. The point being," a pink blush crept around his ears while he continued to ramble, "There's money in this hotel. Whoever constructed it, I'm sure they did a bang-up job."

"I'm not following." His sweet ear blush turned into a full on flush while he stood there. Maybe I'd been wrong about his smirky smile and his womanizer ways.

"The room will stay standing all on its own. You don't need to hold up that beam. It's cemented into the ground well and good."

The joke was cheesy at best. But it did win him a chuckle. He took that as an invitation to continue.

"There's plenty of room at the table. Why don't you join us?"

"I'm fine where I am."

He stood next to me, surveying the room. He ran his hand along his clean shaven jaw, considering something. That slight contact against his skin released the smallest hint of his aftershave, which was something woodsy and natural. His lips twitched while he looked around, as if words were forming there but he didn't want to give voice to them.

"I'll make you a deal." He turned his focus toward me. Those green-gray eyes lit up like he'd just heard the most salacious piece of gossip. "If you come sit with, I'll let you have my cobbler. People fight over Gemini's cobbler when she sells it at the market. It's a pretty big deal, me giving you my dessert."

He extended his hand as if I'd take it and allow him to lead me to where the rest of the group gathered. Unfortunately for him, I'm not a follower and don't eat dessert.

"Unnecessary. Standing is perfectly fine, thank you."

I thought he'd get the hint with that rebuff, but the set of his mouth told me I'd apparently thrown down a challenge he wouldn't back down from.

"Hey, Gem. Can you ask the hotel to bring down some of the captain's chairs from reception? The cushy ones with the oversized arms?"

"What are you doing?" Shock and mortification dripped through my body like a viscous oil, seeping into every dark crevice and strangling me in shame.

"You shouldn't have to stand the whole meeting just because no one realized those damn banquet chairs are uncomfortable."

"I didn't ask you to do that." I railed, "You have no business trying to advocate for someone who you don't even know."

The din of conversation silenced somewhere during our little tete â tete. The sole focus of everyone in the room was us. Gemini and one of the hotel staff rolled in the oversized chair I'd been sitting in before the meeting started.

"I don't need that," I told Gemini, pointing at the object in question. I could feel my throat tightening, and my pulse race. "This is totally unnecessary. I can stand. I'm fine with standing!"

The prosthetic was actually more comfortable when I stood. Sitting made it hurt like hell. It was one of many problems I had to deal with as a result of having only fragments of my femur left intact being stabilized by metal plates.

"I think we should get the meeting started, and Amelia, we're going to be doing a lot of work in our journals today, so it's probably best that you be seated at a table. Is there anywhere in particular you'd like them to place the chair?" Henry asked, pointing to any of the options along the two banquet style tables they had set up. "If there are additional accommodations you require, we can try our best to make sure you have what you need to feel comfortable."

That was the point though.

"Why do I deserve any kind of special accommodation?" I asked.

I already knew what he would say before it was even voiced. My whole body tensed in anticipation. Every time I went anywhere it was always the same.

"You gave an awful lot to this country, just for us to be sitting here today." Butch, an older man in a wheelchair—amputee from the knees down—diabetes, he'd told me last week, signaled to the chair they placed at the head of his fucking table. "You deserve a whole lot more than a cushy chair, young lady."

I didn't deserve a cushy chair. We were all amputees. We all had discomfort in some way or form. And I certainly didn't deserve to be comfortable given all the suffering poor Garcia had gone through. I couldn't think about him right now.

"You've already sacrificed so much." Gemini stood just to my right. I hadn't heard her approach, but she was close enough to rest her hand on my shoulder. "It's just a chair. One that will make it tolerable to be sitting for the meeting today. It's nothing more than that."

"Jesus, guys. If she doesn't want to sit in the chair, I'm sure someone else would be more than happy to." Emmett and I locked eyes, and he raised his eyebrow in challenge. "We have accepted accommodations because of our injuries. But apparently a chair is some kind of knock against Amelia's pride, so let's just move on with our meeting. If she wants to stand in the back of the room, be uncomfortable, and not participate—that's on her. I'm sure her commanding officer or whoever sent her here, will love to hear about how enthusiastically she participates."

Emmett had some balls, I'd give him that.

CHAPTER FOUR

W as it a dick move to challenge her by calling on her sense of duty and obligation? Maybe. But I realized after she threw such a fit when I asked for the chair, that it wasn't the chair that was the problem. It was that I'd called her out for being different. My bad. I realized that after the fact, but the easiest way to get her ass in the chair was to challenge her through her chain of command. At least I hoped so. I didn't know shit about the military. I did know

that she was required to attend and that Henry or Elyse had
to sign an attendance slip saying she was there and
participated. So if I had to pull on that string to get her to
actually be comfortable and not in pain for a two hour
meeting then it was worth it.

"If everyone can turn to page fifteen in your *Journey to
Acceptance* guide, we're spending the day working on asking
for help. Which ironically I think fits perfectly into our day."

We spent most of the meeting interacting with one another
in various pretend scenarios that would require special
accommodations. Amelia continued to stand her stubborn ass
against that pillar, shooting dirty looks my way every so often. I
could see on her face that she was in pain. She shifted
frequently, switching up the way she leaned every five or so
minutes.

"With the last twenty minutes we have left, I'm giving you
a homework assignment." Henry clapped his hands to get
everyone's attention. "In my walk around while you worked in
groups, I noticed something very interesting."

He walked around the room with "hello my name is"
stickers and a sharpie. He stepped in front of each of us and
wrote a word down, sticking it to each person's chest. Mine said
"adapt."

"It's quite interesting. How each of us tries to blend in, but
in different ways. Either we try to shrink ourselves into non-
existence, or perhaps we resist any considerations of our new
normal."

He stopped in front of Amelia and tried to put a sticker on
her. She ducked to the side, grabbing the sticker from his
fingers, instead of allowing him to place it on her shirt. I could
see the word in bold letters, pinched between her fingers. It
said "resist." She caught me looking at her and raised her
eyebrow in challenge. Her assessing gaze felt as if she'd bore

down all the way to my DNA and discovered every weak spot I had.

"For the rest of the time we spend together in this acceptance journey, you will be placed in pairs. Whenever you see your partner acting in a way that matches the word on their sticker, I want you to call "check." This will make them aware of the behavior and hopefully serve as a way for you to find newer, healthier ways of moving into this new stage of your lives. Does that make sense?"

No one nodded their head or showed any form of understanding the assignment.

"So, Emmett here is wearing "adapt" as his word. You'll notice that Emmett rolls with the punches. Whatever challenge his amputation provides, he looks at the situation and just figures out a way for him to move forward. You may think that this is the way we should all strive to be. To adapt to our situations. However, his way of adapting comes from trauma as its source. He adapts because he was never provided the coping mechanisms to ask for help. By adapting, or not making a fuss, he's less likely to be seen...judged...noticed for being different. He'll be paired with Amelia."

I made a mental note to send that guy a cookie basket.

"Amelia is his polar opposite. She resists, even when it's to her own detriment. Her resistance comes in the form of refusing help or accommodation because she doesn't want to acknowledge or act in a way that suggests she is anything other than fully able bodied."

"This is such crap." Amelia ripped her sticker from her chest and tossed it aside. "How does calling us out and criticizing the way we're coping help any of us?"

Elyse tilted her head, appearing to study Amelia, "Do you feel criticized or called out? We're simply trying to raise your awareness of your coping mechanisms. Because you said exactly what we're trying to move you past. You're *coping*. You aren't living. You're not choosing to live a life that accepts and incorporates your status as an amputee into your life plan."

"Coping is moping, accepting is expecting!" Henry added, ticking his points off on his hand as he spoke. "Expecting that your life can be fulfilling and full of the same hopes and dreams you had prior to your accident. If at all possible, I'd like you to find a time outside of our meeting to get with your partner. Whether that's having coffee, or going to the mall, or even the grocery store! I'd like you to experience life with one another in a situation we find ourselves in our everyday norm."

Everyone broke into their pairs, discussing with varying levels of excitement when they would get together ahead of the next week's meeting. Amelia hadn't moved from where she stood. Instead, she had begun to aggressively type something on her cell phone. It was hard to miss all of the "no cell phone" signs that Gemini posted everywhere, indicating that Amelia chose to give a finger to the rules.

"Look, if you want, we can just meet an hour before our regular meeting next week. We don't need to do anything crazy to fulfill the assignment."

"Ah, ah, ah!" Henry sidled up where we stood. "Do you see what you just did, Emmett? In your opening statement about this assignment, you've already signaled to Amelia that her comfort is more important than yours. You told her however *she* wants to do the assignment *you'll* be okay with. I think that is an adapt-accommodate signal, don't you, Amelia?"

Amelia put her phone in her pocket, assessing me in a long pass down my body. Strangely I felt it as if the wind kicked up and pushed through the room. Every hair I possessed seemed to stand at attention while her eyes were on me.

"I think you're right," she told Henry. "What happens now?"

"You tell him, check. And he has to reset, rewind the action you checked him on, and try again."

"I was simply acknowledging the fact that she is traveling nearly two hours to come to this meeting because there isn't anything by her house. How is that exhibiting adapt-accommodate?"

"Would you like to explain it to him, Amelia? I prefer to have the two of you engage in dialogue about checked behaviors without me getting in the way."

"It's a check, *Emmett*, because you opened with an immediate idea on how to accommodate me to make me feel comfortable. And in providing that comfort, you're hoping I agree to your terms."

Henry nodded and gave her a thumbs up. Annoying. At least my eye roll stayed caged behind my eyelids.

"Her refusal to participate and disengage by picking up her phone, then, would be a *check* on resisting also if I'm understanding the assignment correctly?"

"Yes, that is definitely resisting," Henry agreed.

As soon as I said it, I felt like a child. Who does that? Call someone out so that the spotlight shone on someone else. Amelia clearly didn't appreciate my actions either. She directed a very dramatic eye roll in my direction with no shame.

"And how would she rewind that action and move towards acceptance and away from resistance?"

"That one seems much more obvious than mine was. She just needs to be more open. Not turn things down or back out as soon as she feels uncomfortable about it."

"Good, Emmett. Great point. Amelia, if the two of you could exchange numbers, I'd appreciate it. If you do in fact need special accommodation because you live so far away, I'll allow it. Though the intent is to meet somewhere in the beginning of the week to be able to reinforce and observe changed behavior."

Henry walked away to coach another pair, leaving us to our own devices.

"Is there a particular day or time that works better for you?" I asked, trying to think of ways to ask questions without making me seem accommodating.

"What's your number?" she asked, her phone at the ready.

"Three zero five seven seven four nine"

"Great. Look, I need to head out before the snow gets any worse. I'll text you when I get home tonight, and we can figure out a plan."

I was just the slightest bit disappointed that she didn't want to stay and hang out. The resort was fixin' to get all fancy for the big tree lighting festival, and I was sure we'd have plenty to keep us busy. But it is what it is. With the snow you never knew if the system would be just a glancing blow that set down a handful of flurries or if the air was damp enough to turn the storm into a super blizzard.

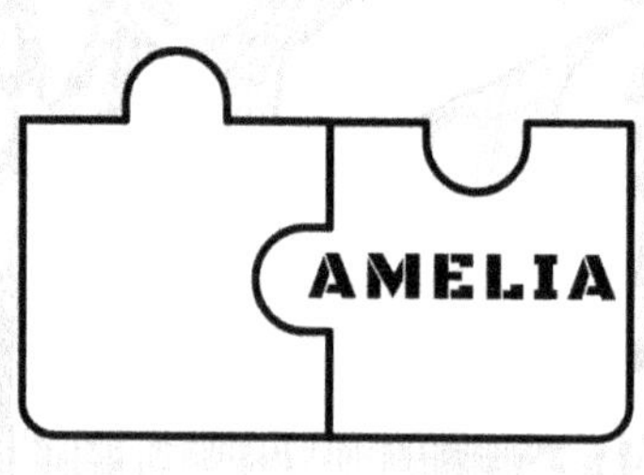

CHAPTER FIVE

Henry and Elyse honestly needed to slow their roll on their self-help kumbaya B.S. Between the *accept and release* mantra, the coping is moping, and this new pairs activity? Way too touchy feely for me. I'm not a touchy-feely person. I'm more accept it, deal with it, and move on.

Though that guy, Emmett, was a surprise. I guess he wasn't the worst partner to have. Even if he did step into business that he wasn't welcome inserting himself into. Like that whole fiasco with the chair. Speaking of that chair fiasco, I'd really done a number on my leg. Sometimes I was too damn stubborn for my own good.

The snow, coupled with the damp air, the overexertion and uncomfortable chairs all converged into waves of pain shooting all the way up my thigh. I silently prayed the roads would be clear all the way back to Haven's Cove. I needed a pain pill and couldn't take one while I drove.

What had been flurries this morning had morphed into big fat snowflakes, which increased with speed and intensity as I tried to make my way out of the city. My cell phone rang, immediately my head flashed to Emmett, and then had me rolling my eyes when I felt a pang of disappointment to see my sister's face on the call screen.

"Annie, what's up?"

"Dad says I have to give you my room!" She burst into tears. "Tell him Meelee. You said being home was just temporary. That you wouldn't be staying long. So, then I shouldn't have to give you my room!"

I could hear my dad in the background, cajoling her. He tried to appeal to her empathy, telling her the stairs were too narrow and hard for me to navigate. She just kept crying into the phone telling me that her room was hers. Honestly, I don't even understand how Annie somehow finagled my parents into giving up the sitting room on the first floor to accommodate her. With eight of us in the family and a fairly small three-bedroom house, we'd all had to share our rooms with other siblings. Now that it was just her, my two younger brothers, Abraham and Abdieso, and our sister Abigail, sharing should have been a piece of cake. Arlan, my oldest brother, Aaron, and Alana were either married with kids, or serving in the military. And then there was me. In the in-between of military servitude and trying to figure out the rest of my life. I'd come home from New

York. There was no point in being close to the base anymore since I was on a medical discharge. I needed to find a path. Given I still had a hard time *coping,* trying to figure out my life's plan wasn't the easiest either.

"Annie, I'm trying to drive in the middle of a snowstorm. I need to focus on the road. Can we deal with this when I get home?"

"No!" she screeched into the phone, my whole stereo system vibrating with the sudden spike in volume. "Dad said I have to have the whole room cleaned out by the time you get home. Tell him Meelee, he's right here. Tell him. If you're going to be gone after the New Year, there's no need for me to move in with Abby. Please. He's right here."

I didn't even have a chance to tell her to put him on. His baritone voice, still tinged with hints of our Guatemalan roots, echoed through my tiny car.

"*Mija,* don't fret over this. She's young. You know how it is."

"Dad, just let her keep her room. I'm fine bunking with Abby."

"Absolutely not. She doesn't even understand the sacrifices that you've had to make and the trials you've endured. Her giving up her room pales in comparison. And I won't have my injured daughter struggling to get up a steep and narrow set of stairs every single day because your mom has allowed Annie too long of a leash."

There it was again—that damn talk of sacrifice and endurance. From my own family even. I didn't want to be accommodated out of some guilt laden sense of duty. In my head at that very moment, a pair of green eyes, attached to a mouth made for sinning, and sandy brown hair surfaced in my brain and said *check.*

"I'm driving right now." I could still see Emmett in my

head, and he raised his eyebrow at me in challenge. "I appreciate what you're trying to do for me. But it isn't worth giving yourself high blood pressure over. We can talk about it when I get home."

"Okay, *mija*. You focus on the road and drive safely."

I looked down to hang up the call, and then my little car slid into chaos.

CHAPTER SIX

"You know ninety-nine days out of a hundred, I'm perfectly content creating comfort food and helping you plan innovative menus for The Tavern. But every once in a while, I feel so constricted." Gemini threw her towel down in frustration, flipping through her notebook over and again. She stood behind our prep counter; her hair tied in a messy bun, and already in chef's whites though they weren't actually white. When we designed the Tuckaway she decided whites didn't fit with the aesthetic of the restaurant, so she'd switched to "an autumnal palate of pumpkin, sage, and teal."

"You have been bellyaching for weeks about how you wish you had more opportunities to show off your fancy skills. What are you waiting for? Or rather, who needs to give you permission to do it? You're part owner of the damn restaurant. Just do it."

Her mouth quirked in tandem with her head tilting and her arms folding. "I'm sorry?"

"You know what, why don't we have a holiday event? We can invite the town, and the people from the hotel! You can create a special menu, maybe Jasper will want to come and showcase his bourbon and whiskey. Finn will see what a huge success that it is going to be—I'm loving this idea, Gem. We need to do this." I squared her shoulder, looking her dead in the eyes. "You need to do this. Give yourself the creative space to explore and innovate."

The whole thing was genius. It checked off boxes for everyone. It showed Finn that the locals were just as interested in this place as the resort guests. Gemini could go crazy with a no holds barred menu to impress the shit out of everyone, and I had a built-in excuse to call Amelia.

"Oooh, we could have carving stations! And like, a Christmas village except it's made from gingerbread and chocolate cakes!" Gemini rattled ideas off, writing down whatever tasks she needed to accomplish in her tiny chef's notebook.

The dinner rush began, and she continued to throw ideas at me and plan the menu in her head, while cooking, tasting, and serving. Finn pushed through the swinging doors that separated the front of the house from the kitchen, his arms full of empty plates. With the snowstorm, a lot of our wait staff had called off, so we were operating with limited help.

"If y'all did less jawing and more cooking, maybe we could keep up with all the people here to eat." He gave the two of us a stern look. Only Gemini got a heated kiss to soften his ornery delivery. Not that I wanted a kiss. But clearly only one of us actually had to deal with him being a pain in the ass.

"Emmett and I are talking through a fantastic idea he had." She tilted her head up to look Finn in his eyes. From where I stood at the stove, I could practically see her shining with excitement.

"Good ideas? From Stubs? Not possible. He lost all of those, along with his sense of humor, when they took his arm." He winked at me before returning his focus back to his woman.

"We're going to throw a holiday party!" Gemini twisted away from his grip giggling, returning her focus to plating and calling out ready orders. "Next Saturday. It will allow the townies to check us out while also giving everyone at the resort something fun to attend."

Gemini answered before I could even open my mouth to answer the question. She handed him the notes we'd compiled just before he'd walked in, overflowing with all the details she wanted to share. I'd expected Finn to smile and tell us we were silly or overboard or a number of things that would show he was mildly annoyed but understood their value. I didn't expect actual upset from him. Especially considering it was Gemini who stood glowing in her element.

"The two of you always over complicatin' things." He threw down a piece of paper he'd been holding. "We live in a simple town, with simple people, who don't need all this fancy shit."

Gemini stood there, frozen, gaping at his little tantrum. But I wasn't going to tolerate that bullshit. Between being lukewarm on the bourbon experience and now outright criticizing a holiday party? I was at a total loss as to where he was coming from. Especially since it was only a year ago when he'd been ready to do just about anything to make sure this bar stayed open, including bringing Gemini in in the first place as a consultant and advisor. I'd been fixin' to tell him exactly what I thought about his shitty fucking attitude when the Sherrif and a couple of the county deputies who'd been eating dinner stepped into the kitchen.

"Sorry to interrupt, but we just got a call that a car drove off the road on I5 before the bridge. The whole town's in the shits with the bridge out and all kinds of spin outs. Finn, can we get your help towing her out?"

We didn't even need to have a conversation about it. Finn and I both got our coats and followed the sheriffs out, while Gemini took over in the kitchen. I asked one of our bartenders to help her with plating and calling out ready orders so she could focus on cooking.

The second we were in his truck and on our way following the sheriff I laid into him.

"Where do you get off, Finn?"

"Where do I get off? Where do you get off? Our tavern is perfectly fine the way it is. We don't need any of this highfalutin' shit. Bourbon tastings and now this pricks fix? What the fuck is a pricks fix?"

I tried valiantly to hide my snicker. Knowing Finn for as long as I had, he didn't like being made to feel unintelligent. By anyone.

"It's prix fixe. It means that for a fixed price anyone can come and enjoy a full menu from appetizers through dessert for fifty-five dollars. That's a fantastic price point for two people. I think it's going to be really successful, Finn."

Finn slapped his hand on the steering wheel. Taking the

opportunity to throw his little tantrum while we waited at a stop light. After a string of expletives and an aggressive rubbing of his hair, he turned back towards me. Surprisingly, he didn't look mad. He looked despondent.

"Hey. Talk to me."

"Aren't we enough the way we are?"

Finn has always been more of the bear just woken up from hibernation type when it comes to feelings and expression of emotion. In a single statement, he pulled back the curtain on his vulnerability. It both surprised me and kind of shocked me.

"Not good enough for what? Gemini?"

"It seems like all she wants to do is change things."

"Finn. She loves you. Like head over heels, in love. She walked away from her whole life in Chicago and Madison to be with you."

"Exactly!" He turned toward me. "She was fresh off her divorce, emotional as all get out, we met and had a crazy kind of courting, and then boom. She's here, and now we're living together. But it feels like every day she's taking on a new project or changing things at the tavern and I wonder if it's because she isn't really happy."

I pointed at the light that had turned green. The sheriff was already a good half block down the road. Finn didn't seem to care.

"You need to talk to Gemini. I won't have the kind of answer you're looking for. I can't speak for her heart, but the way I see it, as an outsider? She's doing all of these things because she wants it to succeed. She's invested because she's in love with you, and this is your venture together. She's pouring her heart and soul into this place, this town, its people—because she wants to be one of us, to care for us as if she were always a townie just like us. Your fear has clouded your common sense."

He ran his fingers through his beard, which was one of his

biggest tells when he thought about what was said. At least he'd realized he'd been standing still and began following the sheriff again. Less than a minute later, he pulled up to an embankment, barely five hundred feet from the entrance of the county line bridge. A red Hyundai two-door sat nose first in a pile of snow. I couldn't stop staring at the car. If they'd slipped just a second later, they would have slid down the gulch and into the river.

"But why would she bring in a bourbon tasting and all these fancy damn entrees? I thought we were trying to be down home and not high on the hog? If people want that kind of stuffy shit they can go and see Duane up the path at the resort."

I think he was quite possibly more stubborn than a mule.

"Finn. Talk to Gemini. And I mean *talk*. Where she speaks and you listen and repeat back to her what she said so you truly listen to what she is *saying*. These types of fancy menus and local experiences draw people in. It draws them in from other towns. It gives the people at the resort something new to try. And townies who still think this is your pop's biker bar get pleasantly surprised with an affordable date night with food on par with the overpriced bullshit slung by Chef Le'sânt up at the resort."

We watched the sheriff walk up to the car. Just as he approached, the door swung open, and a pair of legs peeked out from inside the car. They were legs I was all too familiar with, given they'd been the subject of much confrontation that day.

"Hey, that's Amelia's car!"

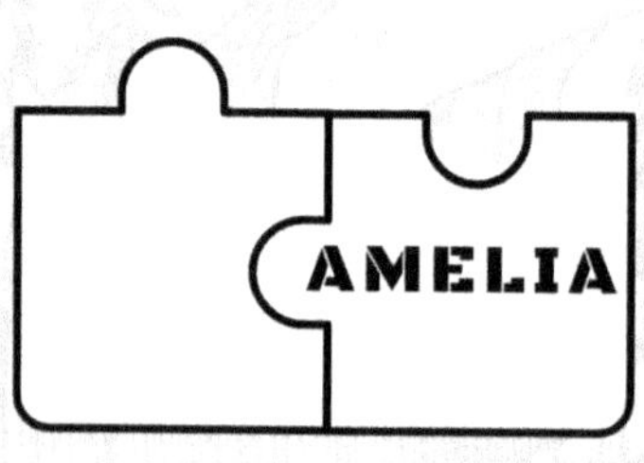

CHAPTER SEVEN

These damn small towns, and all the stupid mountains that surround them. When the weather gets to acting up, you can be buried in minutes. Whiteouts happen frequently up in these parts—even if it melts by the next day in most cases.

"Did you go sliding off the road because you still have a burr in your britches from this morning?"

I heard a voice from a pair of headlights behind the sheriff's car. Emmett's face came into view as he approached the side of my car. There'd been a smart-assed comment on my lips, but seeing him standing there, that devil may care smile on his face and snowflakes disbursed through his hair, made that snotty comment melt right on my tongue.

"Hi?"

"Are you okay?"

I could only nod. This whole day just got stranger. His eyes swept across my face and down my body. Whatever he saw in that brief assessment must have signaled that even though my car looked a mess, I was completely fine.

A tall, bearded guy carrying his towing chain from the front of his car took a stroll around my car before affixing a hook to my back bumper.

"Y'all will need to go have a seat in the sheriff's car. Stubs, I need you to signal me."

"I'm going to help Finn get your car out. Then we'll give you a ride back into town and figure out what the damage is to your car."

He ambled to the back of my car holding his arm up as if to tell that Finn guy not to start towing yet. The sheriff extended his hand to me, helping me navigate the snow and the embankment. I watched his eyes track from it to the dog tags hanging on my rearview mirror that caught the reflection of the truck's headlights.

"Thank you for your service," he said, as he helped me walk to his SUV.

"Shouldn't I be thanking you?" I asked. "Since you too are in the service of protecting."

"Keeping watch over a two-stoplight town is a little different." He chuckled. "But thank you anyway."

"Likewise."

Emmett turned towards me and gave me a thumbs up. I didn't know if he'd overheard the conversation and was proud I'd avoided "resisting" or if he gave me a thumbs up because Finn started to pull my car out of the snow. Whatever the reason, that stupid thumbs up sent my whole circulatory system into overdrive. If it was possible for blood in your veins to smile, that's what mine was doing.

To ADD MORE insult to the progression of the day, the front of my car was all banged up. I'd need some guy named Larry Flynn to take a look at it. I couldn't take it to anyone in either my town or any neighboring town for that matter, because I learned on our drive back to town that the bridge was out, which meant I had to spend the night in Barren Hill.

"Looks like the resort doesn't have any rooms." Gemini put her cell phone down on the table, apology written all over her face. "The snowstorm."

They'd ushered me into a booth in the back of the restaurant, which was perfect given I desperately needed to stretch out my leg. All I wanted to do was take my prosthetic off for the night, sit in a warm bath, and take a painkiller. The pain morphed from mildly annoying to overpowering.

"I'm going to see what Penn can do," she announced, dialing another number. "Shit, he's not picking up."

"I thought he was getting married around this time?" Emmett asked her.

She nearly dropped her phone in panic.

"I don't think so...let me check my calendar." Her fingers tapped furiously on her cell phone screen. "No, Valentine's Day. Jesus, Emmett. Don't scare me like that!"

Emmett and Finn drifted away from the table, getting pulled into different conversations from people at The Tavern. To my surprise, while taking in the ambience of the restaurant, Emmett donned a chef's apron and started working behind the grill.

"He cooks?" I asked Gemini who was focused on sending what appeared to be a text message on her phone.

"Who? Emmett? Yes. That's his job?"

"I can't believe he is a restaurant quality chef, with one arm."

She smiled, putting her phone down on the table.

"You can go back there. He won't mind."

Despite my leg groaning that I'd finally just gotten settled and comfortable, I couldn't resist taking a look. It isn't every day you see a one-armed chef.

"Gemini said it was okay to come back and see you."

Emmett stood in front of a gigantic stove, shaking one pan after another to keep the food from settling and burning. The whole process was a sight to see. Despite only working with a single arm, he commanded that kitchen like an octopus. Between the pans of cooking meat, the sauce he stirred, and the plating, I quickly became mesmerized by his well-choreographed dance.

"Were you coming back here for something specific or just to watch the show?"

I felt the blush rise all the way up to my eyebrows. He busted me, but his voice sounded more entertained than annoyed. I don't know if I would feel the same way if people watched me like a circus act.

"I wanted to see what it was you're cooking because I can smell it all the way out there. And the guy cooking it isn't too bad to look at either."

That last part came out of nowhere. I don't even remember thinking it before I spoke the words. Emmett's eyebrows shot up in, I'm assuming, total shock that something like that would come out of my mouth, especially given I'd been nothing short of an asshole to him all day long. I wish I could have blamed it on the wine, but I'd not had anything but water since arriving at the Tavern.

Emmett didn't respond, rather stirred something that smelled divine in one of his pots, and then grabbed a spoon.

"Here taste this. It's venison stew."

I'd had my share of stews. Whoever decided the menu for MREs loved nothing more than a stew. When I left the army, I swore I'd never eat another stew again. But that one taste of Emmett's stew had me rethinking that.

"Sorry, a little bit dripped off the spoon..."

He reached around me to set the spoon in the sink before swiping his thumb along my chin. I felt that momentary point of contact in my whole body. As if the breaker in my body had been shut for the last three years and suddenly someone flipped the switch, my entire blood stream vibrated with awareness. I think I may have even closed my eyes and moaned. I needed to get out of there before I made a fool of myself.

"Gemini's looking for you. Go keep her company and I'll have the server bring you a bowl. Between this stew and the drop biscuits, you'll forget all the B.S. of this entire day."

"I HONESTLY THINK it's really great that they paired you together." Gemini watched me watching Emmett from where I sat in the booth inhaling the stew he'd suggested I try.

"Oh really? How so?"

Gemini quirked her eyebrow while taking a long sip from her wine goblet.

"Henry's assessment of Emmett is spot on. I've never seen anyone more adaptable to any situation. He's the king of roll with the punches. And I think sometimes he does it to his own detriment. Like he's trying to make himself amenable and personable and that fun, sweet guy that everyone gets along with. As if then people won't notice he's only got one arm."

"It's a little hard to miss."

I didn't mean for that to sound snotty, but the guy only had one arm. How would anyone *not* see that gigantic elephant in the room? Just like me and my prosthetic. The misshapen bulge under my pants usually tipped people off, even if the difference in my gait didn't.

"You'd be surprised." Gemini replied, "The first time I met him I didn't even notice that he was missing an arm. Hand to God. He was so funny and charming—and he and Finn, my partner—" She pointed towards where Emmett and Finn stood chatting while they wiped down the kitchen prep stations. "Those two have such a wonderful friendship that I didn't notice until the next time I met him. And even then, and since, he moves through life as if he has both arms. If something doesn't work for him, he just—figures it out."

She shrugged her shoulders, clearing the last of her wine glass as a period to the conversation.

"I thought you might need these."

Emmett dropped two Aleve in my palm.

"I know it's not a prescription pain pill, but hopefully it at least takes the edge off."

I felt seen in the strangest way. It wasn't the kind of piteous gawking that people did when I walked into a room. Or even the assessing way the V.A. processors looked at you—wanting to help, glad it wasn't them, hiding the discomfort they felt at staring reality in the face. That simple gesture from Emmett however, felt *different*.

"You're as white as a ghost." Emmett's assessing eyes sent that same tingle through me I'd felt earlier. "I think we need to figure out where you're going to stay so you can go to bed."

He turned towards Gemini and the two of them had an unspoken conversation.

"We're up a really steep flight of stairs," she finally told Emmett. "I'm really worried that given the amount of pain she's already in, that might be her breaking point."

Finn wandered close to where we all sat. Both Emmett and Gemini looked at him before back at me. Something unspoken hung in the air. It made me super uncomfortable. It wasn't their responsibility to house me anyway.

"Is there like a St. Vincent DePaul around? They have emergency accommodations for stranded travelers."

"Absolutely not!" Emmett insisted. "My house isn't flashy. There's nothing fancy about it. But it is on one level, and I have a guest bedroom that will give you privacy."

"Oh gosh, I couldn't—" I voiced my opposition at the exact same time Gemini told Emmett what a great idea it was.

"Really, Emmett, I can't impose on you. I barely even know you."

As I said the words, the reality of the situation flashed in my head more than once. I was two hours from home, in an ice storm, with the singular resort all booked out. Where honestly would I go? Even if I had a car to sleep in, the pain in my leg would guarantee I wouldn't get a lick of sleep.

"Finn has a reputation for carrying women up really steep inclines." Gemini looked at Finn and winked at him, blushing. "Maybe we should make him carry you upstairs."

"No, Gem. Finn can give us a ride back to my house, and then when he comes home y'all need to get some things sorted out. I have a perfectly respectable guest room, and it looks like the little resister has no other options if she wants to sleep in a warm bed."

He got up and extended his hand to me to help me out of the booth. That time, though, it didn't feel like he was trying to help a cripple. It felt like he was the gallant knight, escorting a fair maiden.

CHAPTER EIGHT

I never used to be one of those *fate, kismet-y* kind of people. Until Gemini fell—literally—into Finn's arms and the rest was history. Having watched the two of them and their relationship develop over the last year, I'm now convinced that when you throw an intention out into the universe, the universe listens. How else can you explain someone like Amelia just dropping into our laps seemingly out of nowhere?

Except, a small issue. I'd asked the universe for a couple

hours having coffee—and to not be awkward and unlikeable while doing so—not to create a massive blizzard and take out the access bridge. Now she was in my house. In my personal space. Making my skin tingle when she got too close, smelling like warm, freshly laundered sheets in the dead of winter. Crisp, clean, and comforting.

"While it's not nearly as lush as the Echo Creek, I'd say it's probably a step up from an army base."

Shit—first pitch and I'm already taking a wild swing and a miss. Of all the places to remind her of, I choose a fucking Army base. *Bravo, Emmett.* I internally kicked myself, waving her into my kitchen.

"So." I rubbed at the back of my neck, trying to cover for the fact my dumb mouth had just dragged me into a pile of shit. "Let me show you the bedroom. You can set your stuff down. The bathroom is right over here." I pointed to the door next to the TV and dresser. "I'll grab you some towels. It's an accessible tub, you open and close it like you would a car door. Don't start the water till you're in the tub otherwise, it will leak everywhere. But the water heater is on demand, so there's no sitting there shivering while you wait for the water to warm up. Epsom salt is on the windowsill—you know, for the pain."

She seemed surprised that I sussed out how she was feeling. Given my own arm throbbed when the weather got damp and cold, that bathtub could be a godsend. While she nodded and smiled politely while I chatted away, her not saying actual words only made me desperate to fill the silence even more. I needed to get out of that bathroom before I made a total fool of myself.

"There's Penetrex, hemp oil, and arnica in the medicine cabinet. Feel free to pick your poison." I handed her two towels from the linen cabinet, and then showed myself out. "If you need help, just let me know. I'll hang around and watch some

TV just to be safe. It's the room right on the other side of the bathroom, so seriously, just holler if you need me."

I tried to keep an ear out for sounds of distress, but nothing ever came. Eventually I must have dozed off. Some watchdog I was. My phone said it was nearing two in the morning and I was out like a light slumped in my damn La-Z-Boy. I'd just flipped the TV off and turned towards the stairs when I heard what sounded like a whimper coming from Amelia's room. I didn't want to creep her out by leering into her bedroom.

"Amelia?" I whispered, "Are you okay?"

There was no response. I waited another breath just in case she responded and turned to make my way upstairs when I heard it again. The door from the bathroom to her bedroom was partially open, and I could see her, wrapped around a pillow, snuggling it like it was a prize teddy bear. She wore her hair down while she slept. Her curly-cue hair spread out like the mane of a lioness across the pillows. She'd wiggled her way out from under her covers in the middle of the night, the angry jagged lines of her scars catching the moonlight from the window. I traced the angry lines of my own scar, remembering the day at the rail yard.

Amelia's whimpers drew me back into the present. She'd begun to thrash wildly in bed, kicking off the remnants of her blanket before shooting up into a sitting position and screaming at the top of her lungs. All too familiar with night terrors like that, I was action before thought.

"Hey, Amelia." I tried to cradle her against my chest, but the strength in a single arm wasn't enough for someone shackled by the weight of their own trauma. "Amelia." I tried a second time, rocking her back and forth while she writhed and keened.

Desperate to try to raise her into wakefulness without startling her, I hummed the lyrics of "Have Yourself a Merry

Little Christmas." *Meet Me in St. Louis* was on the TV before I'd turned it off, so it was the first song that came to mind. I'd entranced myself in my own humming and rocking, and honestly, I have no idea how long I sat there doing it. Eventually, I felt her tense in my grasp.

"What are you doing in here?" The tightness in her voice mirrored the discomfort I could feel rippling through her muscles.

"I heard you scream." I released my arm and held it up and away, giving her the room to push off me and readjust. "I tried to calm you down. I'm sorry. I just didn't want you to wake up in a strange house, already discombobulated because you aren't in your own bed, and also try to find the line where reality started, and the nightmare faded away."

Amelia wiped her face with the back of her hand, settling against the headboard, before drawing up her knee and resting her chin on it.

"You sound like you're speaking from experience."

"Would you like me to grab you something? Water? Tea? Are you in any pain?"

"Water would be great," she said on a yawn, turning her head against her knee to follow my steps out of the room.

"When the accident first happened," I handed her a water bottle, as well as my bottle of Aleve, which she took and set on the nightstand, "I used to have such a hard time sleeping through the night. Every time I closed my eyes, the whole scene would play out again. It became so bad, I started to become afraid of going to sleep."

"But you say it in the past tense—you don't have them anymore?"

"No, not really. Sometimes." I shrugged, trying to remember the last time I'd even have a night terror. "Certain things knock loose memories. For the most part, though, I sleep pretty sound these days."

"How did you make it through?"

It shouldn't embarrass me. I was a grown assed man, and the fact I found a way to cope and move on should be the key point to this conversation. So what if I needed my best friend to be my safety blanket to scare away the demons.

"Well." I ran my hand through the back of my hair. "To be honest my best friend, Finn, would sleep here. Not together, mind you. We didn't like, share a bed. But I put a twin bed in here over there by the closet. And he slept over every night for probably a month. Anytime I needed anything he'd get it for me. Pain meds, something to drink, help getting to the bathroom if I felt too dizzy to walk there on my own."

Those beginning days had been a haze of pain and sleepless nights. Without him, I have no idea what I would have done. My pa didn't know how to handle caring for an invalid. Especially trying to care for me while at the same time still trying to work at the very place that had rendered me useless in the first place. So Finn came and helped, and my pa did what he knew how to do best. Buried himself in work.

"Eventually as my body healed, my brain started to go sideways. And that's when the terrors got really bad. Normally, Finn sleeps like the damn dead. You send the whole marching band through his bedroom, and he'll wake up the next day humming whatever song they were playing but have no recollection of there being any disturbances in his REMS. But he'd be here at my side every single time I started screaming, crying, or calling for help."

She took a long drink from her water bottle before popping open the cap of the painkillers and swallowing one. Interesting that she moderated her painkiller consumption. The recommended dosing was two capsules for an adult, and yet she still halved her dosage.

"The cases of painkiller abuse amongst amps is like triple the rate of any other group," she told me, setting her water back on the nightstand and inch worming into a horizontal position. "I try to stay really cognizant of even how much over the counter meds I'm taking. It's way too easy to fall into a habit of popping pills because the pain is ever present."

I didn't need to be convinced. She and I rode the same life bus. The only difference being I'd been riding it for a bit longer.

"Finn and Gemini seem like really nice people." Her voice was getting heavy with sleep once again. "I wish I had friends like that. My Army friends—well, that's not a bedtime story. Sometimes though, I wish I had someone to lean on like you do."

"You can lean on me."

As soon as the words were out of my mouth, I felt silly saying them. I'd only just met Amelia a week ago. She didn't need a total stranger, but someone who had the intimacy of understanding her and the longevity of friendship that spanned over decades, like Finn and me.

"If you want, I can hang out here with you while you fall asleep to keep the terrors away."

In the dim moonlight, I couldn't quite make out her full features. I felt more than saw her coffee-colored eyes track down my face, shoulders, and chest and back up again. It was three full beats before she gave me the most subtle nod. It wasn't anything more than standing guard against nightmares, but I felt as if I'd passed some kind of unnamed test.

I lay on my back, arm tucked behind my head. I told her about how we met Gemini last year. How Finn found her at the bottom of the ravine after she took a tumble in flip flops down the hill, and all about how she'd helped us save our restaurant.

"Gemini said that the first time she met you, she didn't even realize you were an amputee. That you were so sweet and charming and acted so normal that it wasn't until later that she even learned you were."

"Gemini was also flat out drunk the first time I met her. So, take that with a grain of salt." I laughed, remembering her sprawled across our pool table, sassing at Finn while he tried to wrap her sprained ankle.

"Can I ask what happened? To you, I mean."

I don't think anyone had ever asked that question of me. Even Gemini learned through Finn about my accident. I'd never told her about it from my experience.

"I honestly don't remember much of the day. I know I'd been trying to release the airbrake on a stalled train so we could shift tracks. Somewhere further up the line something caused all the cars to shift and roll back. I got crushed between two train cars. The kinetic energy that built as the cars smashed against one another became so forceful by the time it reached where I stood that it tore my arm clear out of its socket. The last thing I remember before coming to in the hospital was looking down and seeing where my arm had been."

"I'm so sorry you went through that alone." Amelia reached out in the dark and squeezed my hand, her thumb caressing little circular patterns into my palm.

I got lost in contented quiet, the feel of Amelia's warm body next to mine, and the soothing pattern of her soft breathing. Despite creating a pillow bridge separating the two of us—I didn't want her to worry I'd try any funny stuff in the middle of the night—when I woke up in the morning, Amelia was curled around my leg like a howler monkey, her head on my chest, and arms holding me as if I were a living teddy bear.

CHAPTER NINE

I had a dream about him. Emmett. That instead of drifting off to sleep, he'd rolled me over, kissed every inch of my skin, and cradled me while I screamed out in other ways. The dream was so intense I actually woke up feeling that delicious laxity in my bones as if I had actually come just as I woke up.

"I didn't know what time you normally like to wake up." He smiled at me as I stepped into the kitchen, following the scent of coffee and something cooking on the skillet. "There's coffee right there." He motioned with his chin to the drip pot on the counter closest to me. "Cream and sugar is on the table."

Emmett acted super chill, as if nothing out of the ordinary happened. He didn't bring up my night terrors or the fact that I'd wrapped myself around him like a python in the middle of the night. He'd been right though. Having someone next to me (even if I had invaded his personal space to the infinite degree), allowed me to sleep peacefully for the first time in I have no idea how long.

"Is there anything I can help you with?" I asked, mesmerized by his intricate dance between the stove, the fridge, and the sink.

There were very few items in his kitchen that were actually accessible. I'm not sure why that surprised me so much, but for someone who was so good at cooking, I would have assumed that his kitchen would make his job easier.

"I think I've got everything taken care of." He pulled the towel off his shoulder and bunched it around his fingers to clean them. "We're just doing waffles this morning so it's nothing I can't handle."

His smile dripped through my bloodstream like the butter sliding in the pan he tended.

"There's some strawberries in the fridge, if you'd like some with your waffle."

I opened his fridge and couldn't help but chuckle at how many plastic containers there were full of seemingly random objects: tomatoes, pickles, applesauce. All of them neatly stacked, labeled, and dated.

"The strawberries are in the drawer to the bottom right." Emmett called to me from the stove. "And if you want whipped cream, there is a container of cream in the door."

Embarrassed I'd been snooping, I grabbed the items in question and took them to the table.

"Can I ask you a potentially personal question?"

He set the waffles on a platter between where he set a plate for himself and where I sat. I watched while he puttered around making the whole breakfast picture perfect, setting out coffee and juice along with the waffles and fruit.

"Sure, sugar, shoot."

He took a piece of bacon and took a bite, smiling at me between chews.

"Your kitchen seems so normal."

I lacked an ability to finesse. Blame the Army. Everything about being enlisted was straight and to the point.

Rather than challenge what I said, he pulled his phone out instead, resting it on a little cell phone holder on the table and pulling up YouTube.

"Finn and I have been hosting a YouTube channel for about a year now. At first we did more slapstick like "oh look Finn's a grumpy asshole and I'm the cute charming one." He winked at me with a wide, toothy smile on his face. "Eventually, though, as the channel picked up steam, there were so many people who have been affected by amputation like us, that have reached out to tell me that seeing me finding my way around the kitchen with just one arm, is something that keeps them motivated. He stood and collected our plates, bringing them to the sink. I followed behind him. The least I could do was help him wash his dishes after making such an amazing breakfast.

"And so," he looked around his kitchen, his eyes bouncing from stove to walls and around the room, "I feel like I owe it to those people to see you don't have to upend your whole life in order find happiness as an amputee."

"You adapt."

I handed him a dried plate for him to put away. Our fingers brushed against one another, and you would have thought I'd been shocked by a taser the way my body jumped at the contact. Emmett brushed his fingers along mine a second time, as if trying to get me to react the same way a second time.

"I guess Henry knows me better than I thought."

His lip quirked in a smirk, his eyes tilting up as if considering the world's most complex problems. Adorable. It was the only word I could describe his playful, seemingly adaptable personality. The room felt as if it shifted, the mood went from playful to oddly sensual. Between the previous night's congenial conversation, his care and concern over my well-being, it rolled like a blast of warmth within me, pushing me towards Emmett's lips. I could smell the sweet sugar of the syrup on his breath, and the pine scent of his soap.

"So, looks like the bridge is gonna be out till at least Monday afternoon, possibly even Tuesday."

Finn and Gemini pushed through the backdoor of Emmett's house, breaking the crystalline magic that had surrounded us. They both stomped snow off their boots on the carpet by the backdoor before unraveling their scarves and hanging their jackets on the coat hooks. Neither looked any the wiser that they'd just interrupted an almost kiss between the two of us.

"Wait. I thought it was just ice on the bridge. Won't it melt when the sun comes out?" I asked, returning to the kitchen table and my cup of coffee.

"Apparently the snow collected up in hilltops and slid down, creating a major avalanche. We got more than nine inches yesterday! Can you believe it? That storm came in from out of nowhere." Gemini accepted a cup of coffee from Emmett, smiling at me when I passed her the cream.

Of all the times for that damn county line bridge to get taken out by a snowstorm. The winter season had barely started. It wasn't supposed to snow heavy for another month, minimum.

"There's a Wal-Mart just on the other side of town." Emmett took a seat across from me, "Once we're done here, I can take you over there so you can get some clothes or whatever."

I avoided big box stores. Not because I had any kind of objection to them, but they were so big. The shiny, over-waxed floors were exhausting to traverse while also focusing on staying upright and not slipping. My older brother, Arlan, was always on my case for not bringing a cane or walker with me when I went shopping to stay steady. I already had a giant metal leg for people to stare at, I didn't need any other billboards to draw people's attention.

"It's fine. I don't need to go. I'm good."

Emmett's lip quirked in tandem with his left eye shuttering, as if by staring at me through just the right one, he'd gain some clarity on some deep thought-provoking philosophy.

"Check, darlin."

"I'm sorry?"

"I said check. Want to rewind that comment for me, and tell me why you're refusing help when it's being provided to you?"

"For one, it's still snowing. I don't want you putting yourself in harm's way for an extra set of clothes."

He stood, gathering his opposing shoulder in his hand, head tilted and an obnoxious gleam in his eye that said he was enjoying this stupid little game way more than he should be. I made a mental note to pay more attention to him. Surely, he'd done things I should have been calling check on too.

"I have a truck with four-wheel drive, and it's less than two miles away. If that's the only objection, then I think we can be on our way."

"It's snowing," I told him.

"Yes, you mentioned that already. Four-wheel drive. We're all good."

"We're not. I don't need to go, okay?"

"Sugar, last I checked, Henry said we were supposed to use this method so that the two of us could see the ways we weren't moving towards our self-acceptance journeys. We're gonna finish this conversation. So, let's try again. You said it's snowing. What is it about the snow that has you deciding to exist in the same clothes for potentially three days rather than come with me to Wal-Mart? Are you tight on money? I can cover you."

"My finances are perfectly fine. I don't need your charity."

The words came out much harsher than I intended, but I refused to feel bad for it. He raised his eyebrows at me but refrained from saying anything further. We were locked in a visual game of chicken, and I wasn't going to look away first. I was about to cock my head and cross my arms when his look softened and his eyes went really wide.

"Is it me? Did I do something last night that made you uncomfortable? I'm sorry if I misread the night. I only stayed in your bed because I wanted you to get a decent night's sleep."

Finn and Gemini both became really invested in making the most complicated cups of coffee known to man. Especially considering there was only cream and sugar out on the table. Finn nodded at Gemini, cocking his head towards the living room, like we actually needed privacy.

"Emmett, stop." I held my hand up. "Nothing happened, guys. I had a night terror. Emmett came and laid with me so I wouldn't be afraid. That's it."

"I'm plum out of guesses." Emmett set his coffee cup down and placed his hand on his hip.

"Gemini, would you mind taking Amelia to Wal-Mart to pick up a few things? If she's staying another night, my guess is she probably wants clean clothes and maybe some personal items."

"Jesus! I don't need to go to Wal-Mart. What part of 'don't worry about it' has missed your comprehension?"

I regretted snapping at him as soon as the words projectile out of my mouth. He'd wound me like a viper with his continual need to "check" me. I definitely wasn't used to other people asking me to explain myself, what I said, or my actions.

"The part that knows you're full of shit."

Gemini tucked her phone into her pocket and ducked into the crossbody strap of her purse.

"Look, Emmett, I know you're really invested in this practice scenario from Henry, but how about we just press pause on that, huh? I have a couple things I need to get anyway. Finn saw a movie he wants at the Redbox. We'll just all go. How does that sound, Amelia?"

Given Emmet set me to full boil, I honestly didn't want to do anything. But, since I was being forced to go, I tried to compile in my head a quick list of things that I definitely needed.

"Are there any smaller stores that carry necessities?" I asked as Finn held my hand as I tried to swing up into the backseat of Emmett's truck with Gemini.

"Not in the city limits, unfortunately." Gemini replied, snapping her seatbelt. "The Target is in Mammoth Slope, which is across the county line bridge."

"Wal-Mart is it within the basin. Other than like the Pack 'n Sack and a couple local stores. But they won't have clothes and toiletries."

Finn chimed in, pointing towards the small downtown area we drove through. The downtown area was like any other mining town turned ski and hiking destination—very similar to

Haven's Cove. A sleepy downtown with a pharmacy, a local grocer, a two-screen movie theater, and a thrift shop.

"I think that Emmett is so used to just dealing with his disability, he forgets that not everyone has had the same experience as him."

Gemini looked out the window, tracking the pair of men as they slipped and slid through the snowy mush on their way inside the store.

"I really appreciate this." I pointed toward where Finn stood waiting for Emmett to catch up to him on the curb. "I wouldn't have been able to get through that without serious effort. And then I'd be afraid the whole time we were inside that I'd slip and fall and break something."

"I completely understand." Gemini turned toward me. "And this may be overstepping, but Emmett is a really good guy. He would have understood if you'd just told him that you were afraid you'd hurt yourself in the snow."

Able bodied people didn't understand. It wasn't as easy as that. So many follow up questions came along with that. "Is it the parking lot you're concerned about? I'll drop you at the door. Oh, you're worried about puddles inside? Let me find you a wheelchair. Oh, there's none available. Just hang out here and I'll try to find you one at customer service. They don't have any. How about you try to just walk really slow and I'll hold your hand." The scenario didn't end. And in everyone's desperation to be *helpful* and *accommodating* the trip would end up being frustrating and exhausting.

I opened my mouth to try to explain further but Gemini continued, "I know I don't understand, and you and I barely know one another. With him, when I say something he doesn't agree with or the reply is "Gemini, you don't understand", I tell him to help me understand. But I get it. With him and I, it's different because we're friends and business partners. I do want to be cognizant of the trials though, so I hope eventually you'll entrust me with it."

Her cell phone chirped indicating a text message.

"Finn wants to know if you want him to grab you some underwear. He said it wasn't on your list."

My whole face heated to a temperature I'm certain rivaled the surface of the sun.

"I left it off my list because I didn't want a complete stranger buying underthings for me. I'll just go commando with the leggings. It's fine."

Gemini giggled, blushing. "Probably TMI but Finn loves when I go commando with leggings. Sometimes I'll do it on Sundays when we serve brunch at The Tavern—because it's a short day, like four hours tops. He goes crazy knowing I'm walking around the restaurant with nothing but a thin pair of pants."

She giggled covering her face with her purse.

"Sorry, sorry! There are hardly ever any women around here. I guess my friend-o-meter got ahead of itself. My sister still thinks I'm about to shave my head and buy a tambourine, so she hasn't exactly been the best person to talk to about my relationship."

"I'm sorry, shave your head and buy a tambourine?"

"Oh—yeah. Sorry. Last year when I met Finn, I was just fresh off my divorce. I came here on a vacation and fell in love. I went home for a few months, realized I'd found a piece of myself I'd lost here in Barren Hill and came back to live permanently. Tami—my sister—watches too many true-crime shows on television and worries I moved too fast for a normal human to process romantic feelings and therefore believes I'm in a cult. So welcome. I'll teach you the secret handshake and tambourine solo tonight around the fire."

She texted Finn back, I'm assuming, that I did not in fact need underwear.

"So, Emmett made you breakfast this morning, I hear?"

Her voice sounded totally casual, but the question felt different. Weighted. Like having him make me breakfast held some kind of special significance I wasn't aware of.

"His confidence and ease in the kitchen are really something."

Gemini nodded, smiling in the direction of the entrance to the store. Finn and Emmett had begun the cautious slip and slide back to the truck. The pair carried on as they walked, Emmett kicking slush in Finn's direction and Finn lobbing miniature snowballs collected from the back of the cars towards Emmett.

"Does he have anyone else that lives with him usually? Like if the storm hadn't struck?"

"No. His pa died a few years ago. His mom died in childbirth, and he's got no siblings unless you count that man child presently smashing a fistful of snow into his face. Why do you ask?"

The two of them carrying on pulled a giggle from me. Despite only having a single arm the two of them interacted with one another as if there was nothing wrong with Emmett at all. Seeing that freedom, how he somehow had achieved the normalcy I so desperately strove for each day, tinged my insides with the slightest bit of envy.

"Everything he uses, from canned condiments to shortening—they're all in these gigantic, oversized cans. The kind you'd get at like Costco or something similar. And if it's just him, I can't fathom why he'd buy something so large and risk it spoiling before he could finish using it."

Gemini tracked the two men who continued to make a slow progression toward the car.

"You should ask him sometime about how he became such a good cook." She twirled the string of her hoodie while continuing to watch the men out of the window. "Sometimes your personality traits are born out of necessity."

"I don't understand what you mean," I told her, shifting in my seat so we could converse face to face.

"Henry said Emmett's word is adapt, right? Think about living in a poor mining town that isn't nearly as gentrified as it is now. Where everyone needed to work every day to put food on the table. So there's no money for specialists or occupational therapists, or any of the things that I, having lived in the suburbs of a big city, would assume someone who suffered a traumatic injury would have access to. Emmett had to learn how to do things all on his own. And since most families use items that you purchase in a standard grocery store are made in glass jars, how would someone with only one arm get a glass jar open?"

My experience with amputation was so different from what she described. Most of the military amps I'd met at the minimum had the same standard of care that I did. Along with people within the V.A. who were tasked with helping us navigate through doctors and therapies. I couldn't imagine what it was like for Emmett.

"You can buy an electric can opener at a local store. Restaurants, like the one his best friend's dad owned, had access to economy electric can openers that are built to open those huge economy sized versions of canned foods. If that is what someone gives you to make your life a little easier—you figure out how to work it into your life. And, if you buy one-gallon canned whatever—you adapt. You find new ways to make your leftovers work. Eventually, you become really damn good at what you do."

"Who's really damn good at what they do?" Finn popped

open the passenger door to the truck, passing bags back to us in the backseat.

"I was telling Amelia about what a good chef Emmett is and that he's completely self-taught."

Emmett caught my gaze in his rearview mirror. His ears were bright red and I'm certain that it wasn't all a result from the snowy chill. Gemini's story settled my inner tantrum throwing toddler. He'd only been trying to make me feel comfortable, and I'd been a total asshole. I'd been more concerned about my own discomfort and forgotten that a bunch of people I barely knew were doing everything in their power to make sure that I was comfortable.

"Thank you." I said, "I appreciate you going into the store for me. The snow and ice make it really hard to get around with only one appendage that can feel things like slick patches or gathering water."

"Of course." His whisper of a smile and slight blush softened my inner grinch even more.

CHAPTER TEN

The Christmas Tree lighting was one of my favorite events. Growing up, the resort hadn't yet been built, so the tree lighting happened in town square. But when the resort came, the town agreed to move the lighting to their property. There was more room, which meant more people could enjoy it.

Most of the vendors weren't able to get into town, so the Christmas village was not much to write home about, but despite the headaches the snow brought it sure did make it seem like Christmas everywhere. Gemini and Finn must have kissed and made up, since he was at a stall selling spiked cider and other holiday themed spirits, while Gemini had an entire bakery's worth of holiday treats.

Finn even co-opted the town's snowplow to make sure that the entire area around the Christmas tree was fully accessible, including straw to soak up any melting water, anti-skid rugs that the resort used in the summer around their pools, and salted walkways. All of that additional effort meant that Amelia could join in the festivities without worry. Watching her laugh and carry on with Gemini at their booth, made it evident she was doing just that.

She saw me looking at her and grabbed another cup before approaching.

"I didn't get to tell you earlier, but I appreciate everything you've done for me."

She handed me the cup in her hand. A cautious sip told me it was a hot chocolate with Bailey's in it. Based on the slight flush across the apples of her cheeks, and the loose smile, hers had Bailey's in it as well. The kids' choir finished up its rendition of "Santa Claus is Coming to Town," which typically signaled the arrival of the big guy to come plug in the lights. Unfortunately, Elmer Akins from Mammoth Slope had been playing the resident Santa for the last few years, and he along with our Santa costume were stuck with him on the other side of the bridge.

"It's really no big deal, Amelia. I just wanted to make sure that you had what you needed for the weekend."

"I know." She sighed, taking another sip of her cocoa. "I shouldn't have acted that way. Big stores and snow scare me. I had a really bad fall right when I first had my leg amputated. Real bad—and everyone stared and gaped but didn't offer any help. It was just—" She closed her eyes and pressed her fingers against her forehead as if the act alone could banish the memory from her brain.

My arm—the one that was missing—must have received some kind of directive from my brain to offer some form of comfort to her. I realized too late that she saw the failed motion, and blushed. She placed her hand on my shoulder, the one that had just misfired.

"Even those of us who have seemingly gotten used to this life have moments where our bodies forget." I tried to cover my embarrassment with a soft laugh that felt artificial even to my ears.

Rather than comment on the misfire, she looked up at me and cupped my face, running her thumb along my cheekbone. The pink in her cheeks deepened to red, as realization lit her eyes that she'd touched me in a rather familiar way. The moment she pulled her fingertips from my face, I felt their loss. Where she'd transferred some of the warmth of her fingertips just a moment earlier, suddenly felt the icy chill of winter.

"Sorry," she stuttered, hiding her discomfort behind a sip of hot chocolate. "I have no idea what possessed me to do that."

Her sweet smile, the perfect magic that was the tree lighting, my general attraction to her—whatever it was— I couldn't resist the siren call of her lips a second longer. Already short one arm, I tossed my hot cocoa as close to the garbage can as I could in the heat of the moment and kissed her. Kiss is the most boring word for something that lights you up from the inside. Feeling her soft mouth against mine was like the excitement of New Year's Eve and Fourth of July, combined with the comfort of celebrating a special occasion with your favorite people. I didn't want it to end. A bunch of snickering kids pulled me out from my haze. I'd forgotten the choir had been in the midst of wrapping up their concert.

"If you take his leg and her arm, they make a full person," some little freckled-face boy said, as he pointed toward us and laughed.

"He's a kid." Amelia's hands tensed on my bicep, obviously feeling me fixin' to give him an ear boxing. "There's no point. Just ignore him."

"Listen, you little shit," I snapped, losing my cool faster than I thought I would. "She lost her leg fighting for your freedom. You're all of what, eight? So you don't understand much of that implication. But when your mama picks you up, I'll be damn sure to tell her how you disrespected a disabled veteran."

He shouldn't get a pass just because he was a little punk. Just then she kissed me, and all thoughts of him flew out of my mind. In all the years since the accident, there were few times I'd actually been upset and wished for my arm back. When my pa was dying, and I wanted to hold him so he wouldn't be scared. Last summer at the wedding when everyone was dancing slow and close and I sat at the bar watching and wishing, and right now. Despite Amelia's curly hair being tucked up into the hat we'd bought her, and her arms doing the hugging, I wanted a second hand to feel and explore. To enjoy the little shocks of pleasure each fingertip felt caressing down her coat. To feel her soft skin, hold her jaw while I kissed the breath right out of her, and enjoy the tingle of her hair in my hands.

"So—is this tree thing something that always happens?" She giggled, running her fingertips across her lips.

"Actually, no. When we were kids, they had a lighting in town square. But this?" He pointed towards the tree and all of the decorations. "This didn't start til the resort came into town.

If the bridge hadn't been out, you'd have met Santa, the reindeer, gone shopping in the Christmas village, and I believe I heard they were going to have a Ferris wheel and horse drawn carriages this year. Growing up though, we didn't have much of anything in these parts. It's nice though. I like it. What about over in Haven's Cove?"

"There is a big lighting in the town square. It's cute, charming. It was something we looked forward to when we were kids, especially. It was the only Christmas tree we'd have."

I guess she and I had more in common than I thought we did.

"There's poor," she explained, "and then there is hill poor. We were *hill poor*. With eight kids on a miner's salary, we were lucky to each get a new sweater my mom knit or some school supplies from the church Christmas collections."

Suddenly our entire session with Harry yesterday made sense in the most crystalline way.

"Wow. I can't believe Harry was right," I told her, unable to stop the entertained chuff at Henry's spot-on assessment. "Your abject horror at the suggestion you'd need any kind of help. It's kind of interesting that you learned to reject even before your accident."

"I wonder if my coping strategy isn't actually reject, like Harry thinks."

She almost looked relieved. That look, the rounded eyes and the downturned lips that morphed into the barest hint of a smile, made me sad. It told me that she thought having a rejection mentality meant there was something wrong with her. Not just that she hadn't ever learned another way to deal.

Of course, thinking about her sent the largest lightning bolt of realization up to my head as well. I always had been the one forced to adapt. Even as a kid and in the most basic of situations. I had no mom, it was just me and my pa. While he worked to make sure I had a roof and food and clothes, I needed to learn to roll with the punches. Sometimes we'd only eat white bread and hot dogs til payday. Other times I'd have to go without a new pair of shoes because something happened with the truck, or taxes, or reduction in hours at the rail yard. Rolling with the punches was the name of the game in Barren Hill.

"I think it's just more amplified," I told her, realizing she'd been waiting for a response from me. "Because when you were a kid you hated having to depend on other people's kindness to have your needs met. It became a source of shame. So now you equate shame with needing help."

"If I hadn't seen you in action in your restaurant, I'd swear you were some kind of therapist. My care coordinator is gonna flip when I tell her this!"

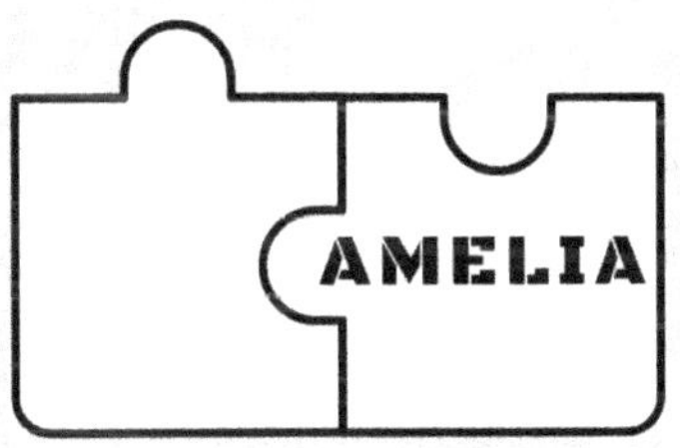

CHAPTER ELEVEN

We'd upgraded to kissing. I don't know where in the arc of the two days spent in Barren Hill we'd graduated to this point, but I wasn't going to question it. Emmett was a ten out of ten in the kissing department. I wanted more.

I basked in the pleasant warmth of the town. I made two new friends in Finn and Gemini and enjoyed the sweetest Christmas tree lighting. I was high on life and probably a little more relaxed than usual thanks to the Bailey's in the hot chocolate. After the tree lighting and the singing, Emmett and I stole away into the resort to "warm up," and "rest my leg."

"Over here, by the fireplace," Emmett suggested, directing me toward a settee tucked out of the way of the main thoroughfare nearest to the elevators and restaurants.

"C'mere," he pulled me against him, as we collapsed onto the settee.

I couldn't stop touching him. Feeling the ridges of his chest beneath his coat, the abrasive scratch of his five o'clock shadow, and the lush warmth of the pouty lips I couldn't get enough of. Each kiss wound me tighter. Suddenly, I wanted more. More tongue, harder kisses. I wanted to give as much as I took. And I needed to feel it all. To drown in the heady haze that spun me in a web of need.

"Amelia," Emmett crooned, "We should stop but I can't get my body to agree with my brain."

I couldn't get out of my jacket fast enough. While fully aware I was in a public place, I wanted to feel the heat of his hand closer to my actual skin. A single kiss morphed into two, which turned into a slide of tongue and a shift in positions.

Emmett's hand was everywhere. Under my shirt, on my back, holding my neck in place while he plundered my mouth. I had no idea how I could feel completely consumed by him with only a single arm eliciting all of that sensation on my body.

"Just five more minutes," I told him, between heady kisses. "They're going to start looking for us soon."

One minute, I joyfully pressed against Emmett, the pressure of the growing ridge in his jeans getting ever so closer to a place that had long sat dormant and ignored. Seconds later, fire shot through my core. A pain so intense it stole my breath from me in the exact opposite to what had occurred with Emmett moments before. The sudden onslaught sucker punched me right in the solar plexus. It made it hard to think let alone form words. I didn't even know where the agony centralized or why it tore through me with such ferocity. The shock and speed of its appearance yanked me into a flashback of the early days in Landstuhl. The days when anguish was the only feeling I knew, and my brain left me rudderless in an ocean of torment and confusion.

CHAPTER TWELVE

I t made no sense. One minute we were all smiles and giggles, then we were heated kisses which were unexpected but in the best way. And now, Finn stood in my guest room grabbing Amelia's things.

"She's embarrassed, that's all," Finn said, gathering the newly purchased clothing that she'd been considering before leaving for the tree lighting. "Something happened—like a flashback or something—and she panicked. I'm sure once she calms down, she'll call you."

Finn and I had been friends for a really long time. So long in fact, we may as well have been brothers. Of all the things that had happened in our lives, losing our dads, his mom running off to god knows where never to be heard from again, me not having one, girls in high school, women as we'd moved through our twenties, me losing my arm. Through all of it, I'd never seen pity in his eyes.

Concern? Sure. A protective streak that sometimes felt like he was babysitting me? Probably more times than I cared for. But pity? That was something Finn had never done. Except right now. It wasn't even the jutted lip that looked like a frown. It was his fucking overly empathetic eyes I couldn't look at. They said plenty. Like "sorry, bro. I know I made you step out of your comfort zone and told you to swing for the trees with a girl and now you struck out in the most glorious way."

"It doesn't make any sense, Finn."

"Post-traumatic stress doesn't make sense, Stubs. It takes your reality, crumbles it in his hand, gives you the finger, and then slingshots you into an alternate reality."

"She had a really bad nightmare last night," I told him.

"I'll let Gem know to keep an ear out."

"Just tell her I'm sorry."

Finn nodded at me before pushing into my screen door and heading towards his truck.

Me: I'm sorry.

I texted that night while I lay in the bed we'd shared the night before. After Finn left I'd just sat here, trying to figure out where things went wrong. Tried replaying the whole evening to find where the landmine had been.

Me: I'm here, whenever you want to talk

I stared at the screen for an eternity willing those stupid response dots to appear. They never did.

***

"You've been moping around here for two days." Gemini looked up from our planning binders. "Just call her."

"She is the one that freaked out, Gem. Shouldn't I give her the space to sort through whatever she's going through?"

Our holiday dinner was in less than three days, and I didn't feel any kind of holly or jolly—in fact, I wished the holidays were already over.

"She must think I did something wrong. Otherwise, why wouldn't she call? I bet she's upset with me for some reason. I shouldn't have suggested we go inside. I moved too fast. We don't even know each other that well."

Gemini wiped her hands on a towel and threw it on the counter before coming around the counter and squaring my shoulders so I was forced to look at her.

"When Finn and I got into a fight on Saturday,what did you tell him?"

I hadn't realized Finn would have told her about our conversation. The revelation surprised me in the best way.

Knowing that he was as head over heels for her as she was for him settled me. It was a weird comfort knowing that he would always have her by his side.

"I told him to stop being an asshole with his head up his ass."

That pulled a full-fledged guffaw from her.

"Don't pull any punches, Emmett." She continued to giggle. "I mean you told him that he needed to talk to me to know what I was thinking, right? That you couldn't act as an advisor to my insight because you weren't me. Right?"

"I hate when you're right, you know."

She laughed and pulled me into a hug. "It's your advice. I'm just repeating it. So you hate that you're right and have to follow your own advice."

I realized that even though I'd thought about inviting Amelia to the holiday party, I never actually had. So many other things happened I never got around to mentioning it. It was the perfect follow up for a phone call, which went straight to voicemail. I tried not to take it personally; surely there were plenty of reasons I'd get her voicemail with no ring. She could be on the other line, or her phone could be turned off or have no service. Dozens of reasons.

"Hey, Amelia, it's Emmett. I'm calling to check in and see how you're doing. I'm a little worried. I hope you're okay. If you don't have any plans on Saturday, we're having a holiday party at The Tavern, and I'd love for you to come. I know Gemini would love to see you as well! All right, give me a call when you have a second."

Hopefully I didn't sound as pitiful and desperate as I felt leaving that message.

Checking in with my RCC ranked around my least favorite activities. Especially since the last time I met with Pam she was nothing but stone faced business and tough love. I brought her a cup of coffee from the Dunkin Donuts across from the V.A. as my attempt at a peace offering. You'd have thought I'd offered her a trip around the world with the reaction I received to bringing her that coffee.

"I see you've attended two amputee support meetings.

That's great!" Pam began, looking over my file, making a show of taking an appreciative sip of her gifted coffee.

"And *I* see," I pointed towards her windows with my own cup, "that you added holiday decorations to your window in addition to ornaments on your little pink tree."

She looked up in surprise. Maybe she thought I didn't pay much attention to what her office looked like? Who knows? Honestly though, how does one not notice the surroundings in an office that you see once, sometimes twice a month?

"Tell me about what you've learned so far in those meetings." Her pen was at the ready, waiting with barely contained excitement, to write down every word I spoke regarding those meetings.

"For the most part, they're pretty cheesy," I began, trying to find a comfortable position in her guest chair. "There's a lot of touchy feely shit about what you do when you feel embarrassed, or if people are staring at you. Though Henry—he's our leader—partnered us up this past week so that we could point out to each other when we acted in a way that reflected the verbs that he assigned us."

"Verbs?" she asked, pushing her glasses further down her face to look me in the eye uninhibited by her readers.

"Yeah. He said that all of us have ways of acting as part of our coping mechanism. For example, he said I'm resist, and my friend, Emmett, is adapt. And we discovered that it's not necessarily that we have resisted and adapted as a result of our amputations but that we use those as our coping mechanisms because *that* is what we were taught. It's our learned behavior, like since childhood! So, we resist and adapt because it's our comfort in an uncomfortable situation!"

"Your *friend Emmett*. This is a development that I want to hear all about. Especially since according to you, he is your literal counterpoint. Is he young? Single? Oh my gosh, Amelia, this is a rom-com desperate to be written."

If only she wore an oversized hand knitted sweater and had pictures of her cats on her desk, she'd make the perfect best friend in this imagined dream world scenario. Alas, she was a government worker all the way down to her style of dress, completely plain and unassuming khaki pants, blue long-sleeved T-shirt, and a navy wrap sweater.

"Pam, focus. Did you hear me? Your little social worker's heart should be singing a swelling Disney song right now. I literally just recognized my own source of trauma and acknowledged that I am repeating patterns of behavior."

"Amelia, that looks like a blush to me. It's not nearly hot enough in here for that to just be a too warm office. You've been holding out on me! And yes, I am thrilled that you and your friend, Emmett," she did those cheesy air quotes and winked at me, "were able to figure out all on your own that you repeat patterns of behavior because they are what is familiar to you. This verb/checking thing is fascinating. I'm making a note to circle in with Henry because I think it's such a great way to make people cognizant of their coping mechanisms. That is a really big step for you. So don't think I'm not jumping for joy, but your friend Emmett sounds like a giant step too... so, tell me about this friend."

Pam and I never really had much of a connection. I came in, told her what was going on in my life and she wrote in her file and sent me to fill out another form or visit another office and have them give me whatever form she needed. This bubbly and excitable side of Pam was something new, but I dug it.

"There isn't much to spill, and honestly I probably fucked it all up anyway."

"You messed up all of what?" She braced her fingertips on the desk and leaned closer. "Amelia Sanchez, you are in here once a month and you sit here with nary a smile on your face, and today you come in here all *oh, I have this friend.* What changed? And how? Start from the top."

I summed up our two meetings and gave her the highlights of our interactions. A surprise even to me that I wanted to tell her about the last two weeks. I needed to unspool it all for someone so they could look at the pile and confirm I was in fact justified in feeling my feelings.

"Then he kissed me. And this shithead little kid told us that together we made one whole body and Emmett got all upset over it. But then I kissed him back and that took it to a whole 'nother level. And by the end of the night, we were sneaking away into the lobby of the hotel and making out in a hidden corner."

She leaned her chin against her fist, braced against the desk. Her desk phone had rung twice while I regaled her with what felt like the most juvenile example of romantic interest between two adults. Based on the way she looked at me, all shiny eyes and toothy grin, my pitiful encounter as a thirty-two-year-old adult was apparently still gossip worthy.

It obviously had been a long while since I dated. Even before riding the rocket that led to my separation from my appendage,I had been pretty inexperienced. The dating potential in hill country was pretty slim, even when you considered sharing a high school with the other small towns in the basin. Then I went to the Army and didn't want anyone to think I was a Betty—a woman just in the army to find a mister, get pregnant, and then exit with benefits—so I kept to myself.

"Something really weird happened actually." I didn't really want to share my embarrassment, but it bugged me. "We were making out; I was super into it. I'm in his lap, and then all the sudden I have this explosion of pain through my entire—um— female region."

"Did he put his fingers too deep?" Pam asked, confusion wrinkling her forehead.

"Pam! No! His fingers weren't anywhere near there! We were in a hotel lobby!"

I looked over my shoulder to make sure no one in the V.A. was walking past her open door while she's asking about me getting fingered.

"I need you to spell this out for me because I don't understand."

Just thinking about Emmett again made me smile. Which, just as it had every other time I'd thought about him, hot on the heels of those sweet tender feelings came the ice bucket of shame drowning it all out again. I needed to return his messages, but I didn't really know what to say.

"We're kissing, I shift on my good leg to bring my bad leg over his hips, and sit in his lap. I'm thinking maybe we'll do a little grinding, you know—sort of a pre show—and the second my body came in contact with his, the whole world went white, the pain was so intense it took my breath away, and then I slingshot back to Afghanistan."

"And then what?"

"I'm not really sure. I know Finn was there and yanked Emmett up off the couch. He thought he'd done something to make me start screaming. I was crying hysterically. Finn was telling Emmett he was going to coldclock him and asking him what the fuck was the matter with him. I had to tell him I was fine, and explain I'd been triggered into a flashback and all that. But by the time I calmed down and found my bearings, I was so embarrassed I couldn't go back to Emmett's place and look him in the face."

Pam leaned back in her chair, chewing on the end of her pen.

"First, I am really proud of you. Last month, there's no way you would have shared any of this with me. Obviously, attending that group, even if it is cheesy, is making you more comfortable talking about feelings. I really want to acknowledge the fact that you're doing the work and I'm seeing proof of that work."

The earnestness in her voice felt like the softest blanket being wrapped around me on the coldest day. It was a relief or a comfort I didn't think I needed. But knowing for once I achieved what was expected of me, it felt good.

"I think you should schedule a consult with your wellness team. I'd probably see if you could have a meeting with both your amp team and your women's doctor. Just to make sure that there isn't anything of concern, you know?"

She turned to her computer and pulled up their internal scheduling system.

"It looks like both doctors have availability in about two hours. Well, wonders never cease. You're actually getting taken care of in an expedient manner." Pam chuckled, writing out my referral to take to processing. "You should play the lottery today. I think you might be the luckiest case I have."

We discussed the flashbacks and nightmares, and she made notes for the mental wellness team. I was sure I would have a few new appointments that would pop up in my chart once I brought my referral downstairs. I had a feeling there was some couch time in my future.

"I think you should call him." Pam handed me the referrals. "You have a couple hours before your next appointment. Plenty of time to tell him what you told me. Think of it as a growing exercise. Report back to me after you talk to him, and I'll finagle some extra eval points for doing it."

"Pam—you play a dirty game."

"I never said I was fair. Just effective!"

I spent the rest of the day at the hospital. While most of that I spent waiting on one doctor or another, between my gynecologist, the orthopedist, and neurologist, they'd uncovered something I would have never expected. Nerve damage. Well, the obvious nerve damage was a given. But the hits kept coming. As if losing a leg wasn't enough trauma, I now got served a plate of sexual dysfunction.

"You see, Amelia, the map of nerves in the human body is both amazing and complex." The neurologist had a non-amputated body up on the screen to show me the road map of the nervous system.

"This nerve," he used one of those stupid red pointers to highlight it on the screen, "is the peroneal nerve. That's the major nerve damaged in a transfemoral amputation such as yours. Especially in a TFA such as yours where the bones became significantly severed. The sticking point with this peroneal nerve is something we are just slowly coming to understand in the fields of neuro-gynecology. Which is the study of the clitoral structure, its vascular structure, and the relationship of the various nerve structures that surround it. Each of these play into how the clitoris responds to stimuli."

They'd lost me. I passively understood. I swear all of these doctors were the same. They all get so caught up in their big brains and medical terminology that they forgot we were people that were just trying to figure out our lives.

"Doctor, please. Can we simplify this for those of us in the room who studied social work and not medicine."

Thank god Pam had insisted she be present as part of my triad of care.

"My apologies, Pam. The resulting nerve damage from the IED and loss of limb, has created a complex overcompensation to your clitoral structure. Which means when it becomes stimulated, it can't figure out what to do with the rush of stimuli. The brain has been telling your nervous system for some time to deaden stimuli to your right leg because there is nothing there. So your body is confused."

"Imagine your nervous system is like a spigot," the gynecologist interjected. Her hair blocked her name tag, and I'd forgotten her name from our initial introductions. "Your amputation has been telling that spigot not to bother diverting water anywhere within this cluster of nerves."

She too pointed onto the picture of the nervous system with another pointer—hers was green. I wondered off hand if they coordinated those. Like did their admins talk with one another and say, "Okay, Bill is bringing his red pointer to the meeting, so Suzy will need to use green or purple."

"But by engaging in sexual activity with a new partner—"

"It was just a kiss." I could feel my face explode with heat. Talking about my sex life in front of four near strangers was not what I'd expected for a Wednesday afternoon.

"The kiss, however, signals the brain to begin the arousal process." The gynecologist continued, "So, your hormones increase, your blood flow increases, which swells the clitoris, which delivers the pleasure signals from your nerves back up to the brain to proceed further and notch up those feelings of desire. The problem is that there is a roadblock somewhere in that pattern. And instead of delivering feelings of pleasure, your nerves are overcompensating and creating a shortage almost. Like if a fuze got too hot and popped in the fuze box."

"So, what's the resolution?" Pam asked, looking between the three doctors, pen at the ready, "or is there even a resolution?"

"Of course, there's a resolution." The neurologist began, "We, of course, want you to have the most normal and healthy life that you can. My suggestion would be to be open and frank with your partner. Both of you will need to be patient as you explore what sexual satisfaction looks like in this new normal. The nervous system is very complex. Nerves regenerate. Sensation you thought was lost comes back."

"If I can interject again." The gynecologist who finally moved her hair off her collar so that I could see her name was Dr. Xiao spoke up. "I realize this is hard to discuss in front of these two male doctors. Sexuality is a very personal and sensitive topic. Being in the Army strips you of a lot of the considerations we provide to non-enlisted patients. However, as an amputee who is presently part of a triad of care, we all need to be present in order to be able to treat the comprehensive issues stemming from the IED. I would say your first steps would be to invest in some warming lubricant, maybe a good spicy book or two, and an open mind ready to remap your pleasure zones. The clitoris is much larger than doctors even twenty years ago understood. So don't be afraid to explore places that either hadn't given you pleasure previously, like perhaps a g-spot. Or even some places that may be considered dirty, taboo, or not for girls raised in certain religious homes. The anus has lots of nerves attached to the clitoral structure as well. I want you to know, woman to woman, there is zero shame in getting to know your own body in all of the ways it can bring you pleasure."

BEING in the Army strips you of most senses of privacy or embarrassment when it comes to most bodily functions. Especially soldiers that are stationed in the middle of a war, in a desert. However, I believe I'd just discovered my limit. Of all the things I had expected to discuss , my anus, lubricant, and masturbation were not anywhere in the realm of things that had entered my consciousness.

Dr. Xiao handed me her business card, as well as a card for a naturopath who specialized in the exploration of female sexuality. I honestly couldn't wrap that meeting up fast enough, and if getting out of there quicker meant taking her pamphlets, so be it. I wasn't sure I'd be looking her up any time soon, but I appreciated that for the first time a doctor treated me like an actual person and not just PFC Sanchez, transfemoral amp.

"Please feel free to schedule consultation time with me if you ever want to talk or need advice."

She also turned over some pamphlets on female sexual dysfunction and a list of suggested "sexual aids" that I could look into investing in. I could only imagine what my mother, father, or any of my siblings would say if they saw any of this information laying around my house. While instinct told me to throw them out right as I exited the building, instead I shoved them into my backpack, intending to look at them at some point when I had privacy and after I absorbed all of this new information.

Other than receiving a very short text letting me know that she was okay, had a string of tests at the doctors, and would see me on Saturday, I hadn't heard from her again. Did see me on Saturday mean at our weekly group? Did that mean at our holiday dinner? Thankfully we'd been so busy prepping for our big night that it distracted me from obsessing over these details and replaying Sunday night in my head over and over again. I worried that between when I'd seen her last and now that she would talk herself out of exploring a relationship with me.

"Damnit!" An entire tray full of lava cake filled ramekins went crashing onto the floor. "Stupid fucking, slippery piece of shit!"

Even throwing the tray in the sink and slamming the oven door shut didn't make me feel any better.

"Here, let me help." Gemini ducked down with her oven gloves on and began picking pieces up off the floor before I could tell her I didn't need her help.

"I've got this," I told her.

"I know you do. But with two of us, it gets cleaned up faster and then we can talk about what's really bothering you."

"What's going on?" Finn walked into the room, spotted us on the floor trying to contain the mess, grabbed a pair of gloves and dove in with the assist.

"Just a stupid off-balance tray. I should have been paying more attention. My wrist couldn't compensate for all the little ramekins shifting. I'm sorry I ruined your trial run, Gem."

"It's just dessert." She went to put her hand on my shoulder and realized it was covered in chocolate goo. "It's nothing that can't be cleaned up and remade."

"I was coming in here to remind the two of you that you still have your support group meeting, and it starts in thirty minutes."

Finn took the broken ramekins from Gemini's hands, kissed her, and told her to go get ready. I watched him walk back toward the bar, call to the servers who were setting up in the dining room, and asked them if they could finish cleaning up the floor.

"Go wash up and I'll walk with you to the resort."

It was a rare occurrence that Finn wanted to just randomly take a walk with me. If he had talking he wanted to do, it was usually right at the bar or on the back porch. We weren't the walking and talking type.

"I know you're all twisted up still." He batted his opening volley as soon as we got outside. "Her leaving was a result of her feeling ashamed over what happened. That's it."

I tried to sound unaffected and detached. "It's fine. We aren't really anything but a couple of friends that got caught up in the heat of the moment."

Even as I said it I could feel the lie weigh heavy on my tongue. I didn't want to just be friends with her. I wanted her to be mine. To look at me the way Gemini looked at Finn.

"You better go back and shower." Finn pushed against my shoulder. "Because that is the ripest load of a shit I've ever heard. You dig her. I know you do, so don't hide from how you feel."

"Finn, it's different for you. You just don't get it."

"Different for me, why? Because I have both of my arms? You think just because you lost your arm you're what? Destined to be alone?"

His words struck like an arrow, fast and true. I hadn't had a real date since I lost my arm. I'd met a few girls on Match or eHarmony, and despite me telling them I was an amp, when they were faced with the reality of that situation, they'd bail. Some of them didn't even make it through drinks at the bar before having somewhere to go.

"Finn, how many women you seen me with in the last ten years?"

He kicked a pinecone on the path before answering.

"The same amount of women you seen me with. None."

"But you could have dated, Finn. You could have joined any of these dating apps and I'm sure you could have had any number of women."

"Maybe, but then I'd have been too distracted to notice

when the perfect one literally fell right into my lap." He chuckled, running his hand through his beard.

"You dig Amelia. It's great that you did her. I love watching you run around like a little infatuated schoolboy with a crush. But Amelia digs you, Emmet. She looks at you the same way. So you just need to go for it, and stop being such a scaredy cat."

"I ain't a scaredy cat." I make an attempt to kick him in his ass but he ducks out of the way at the last minute. "I put myself out there and every woman turned me down."

"Because, you ninny,they weren't right for you. They were getting you ready to appreciate and act on the one that slid right into your life when you weren't expecting it."

Sure. So easy for him to say. Gemini made it obvious from the onset that she was interested in dating him. Amelia didn't want to date. She wanted to figure out her life and finish up her eight weeks of required meeting attendance.

"Have you heard from her since last week?" Finn asked, pulling me out of my musings.

"Yeah, she texted me a few days ago. But nothing else. Like just one short little text that doesn't say much at all."

I handed over my phone to Finn so he could see what she said. He glanced at it, closed down my phone and handed it back to me. We walked in silence for two beats before he spoke.

"Here's the thing. You and Gemini get along so good because the two of you are very similar in your personalities. You're passion and emotion. Me? I'm boring. I like simple stuff. I'm perfectly happy sitting on a boat in the middle of a lake with just me and my thoughts. I think that Amelia is very similar, and her being a vet—it just amplified that part of her even more. Based on how worried she was about hurting your feelings, and the amount of embarrassment she expressed when she was with Gem and me, there is no question in my mind that she digs you hard. I think you're expecting someone to communicate and share like you and Gemini do. But the reason you and me are such great friends, and the reason that I love Gem with every cell in my body—is because we're different. We're puzzle pieces that fit together and complement one another."

Somehow, I got the feeling he was talking more about him and Gemini and less about me. My new, barely sprouted, couldn't even be called a relationship yet, as it was more of an undefined "thing." I'd been so focused on trying to put a name to what Amelia and I had that I missed Finn taking something out of his pocket.

"I'm going to give it to her for Christmas."

An engagement ring? He was going to give her an engagement ring. A beautiful, antique ring with an elegant pink sapphire stone.

"Do you think she'll like it?"

Finn was gruff. Quiet but listened and thought through everything he heard, weighing all information together before coming to a decision. There is no way Gemini would ever not like something he gave her. First because she loved him and thereby would love any gift from him. But Finn also paid attention and kept mental track of cues I would never pick up on. The shift in emotion, the pitch of her voice, the way she arched her back and would stand like a flamingo when she got worn out from standing and cooking for too long. He cataloged it all and would react to her based on his observations.

"She's going to love it. It is perfect for her."

"I hope so. I'm nervous that she isn't going to want to get married so soon after she just got divorced. But I can't imagine not being married to her. Every time she introduces herself as Gemini Tate, I realize how badly I want her to introduce herself as Gemini McKay."

"I get what you're saying, but I think as far as her

professional identity she'll probably stick with Gemini Tate. Just preparing you for that. Because, as a chef, your name is your brand. And well, she just had to go through a massive rebranding to go from James to Tate. I'd suggest not hitting the gas on the Tate to McKay."

Finn snapped the ring box shit with a *clack*, nodding to signal he heard me.

"How did I make it here before the two of you?" Gemini called from the door to the resort. "You left ten minutes before I did!"

"We decided to take the scenic route," Finn joked, holding open the door so she and I could walk through. "I check the ravine every so often to make sure no one else is out there traipsing around in flip flops."

AMELIA WASN'T EARLY for our group like she'd been the last two weeks. Maybe her car was still with Flynn and she'd needed a ride to group. I had my phone out to text her when I saw her out of my periphery come into class. Henry—or maybe it was Gemini or Elyse—had us all sitting in the oversized captain's chairs this week. She surveyed the room, saw where I was sitting, smiled and bee-lined right toward me. That action alone settled my jitters.

"How are you doing?" I whispered, when she sat down.

"I've been thinking about you," she replied, a warm smile spreading across her face. "I'm sorry that I haven't gotten back to you. Between what happened, and sorting out my car, and the doctor's appointments..." her hand went to mine and that brief moment of contact had a tide of warmth lapping through my bloodstream. "I'm really sorry that I freaked out on you last week. Sincerely "

I opened my mouth to say who knows what, probably a lot of flowery shit about how I wanted to always be the one she could lean on and that I never wanted her to feel embarrassed in front of me when Elyse called to us from the front of the room.

"Emmett, Amelia!" She pointed towards us with the tip of her pencil. "Since the pair of you are so chatty, it must mean that your assignment went well. How about you update us on resist and adapt."

Amelia looked like she wanted to disappear. Eyes wide with panic, she turned to me, speechless. I brushed aside a strand of hair that escaped and had fallen over her eyebrow. Seeing her close her eyes and lean into my hand, shifted something into place inside me. Even if she didn't say anything I knew she was as into me as I was her. I gave her a smirk and a wink before turning towards Elyse. I had no problem being the spokesperson.

"Honestly, I think the two of us made significant strides this week. Not only did we have a couple of instances to interact—with the huge snowstorm keeping her trapped in Barren Hill for the weekend—but we also discovered as we talked about our childhoods that these coping mechanisms we have are actually devices we've used since we were young. For example, I didn't have a mom growing up. And so, as a result of being raised by a single dad, I always had to roll with the punches as they came. When I lost my arm, it was just another punch that I needed to roll with it. Adapting is almost like a comfort behavior because it's what is familiar."

"Very good job, Emmett. I'm impressed with how much the pair of you worked out in such a short span of time. Amelia, would you like to add anything?"

"Well, I'm not really much for group participation. But since I'm trying to act counter to my typical coping mechanism and not resist this process, I'll say that the week has been very enlightening in many ways. Emmett has seen me at my absolute worst this weekend—I got triggered into a panic attack during the Christmas tree lighting. Instead of talking to him and telling him what was going on, I retreated and hid in shame. Resisting once again help from others to get me through.

"I also had my meeting with my monthly care coordinator. Her name is Pam. She was the one that made me come to these meetings. Anyhow, when I saw her, she said she could already tell that I was changing just by how I interacted with her during our consultation. I know that I can be a bit brash. But seeing her yesterday, it was like talking to a girlfriend. It was as if I was hanging out in her living room, and we were having a chat."

"That's great, Amelia, but how does that pertain to our partner work?"

I could clearly see the connection. It irked me that Elyse would be so flippant with what she shared. How did she miss how one influenced the other?

"I shared with her this exercise, and told her about how Emmett and I were putting it into practice. She thought resist was the perfect word for me. Wednesday was a big day for me at the hospital, and having her by my side to help navigate it was a big step for me. Normally I would have just done it on my own. But because of Emmett and the work we've been doing, it was as if he sat on my shoulder whispering 'check' every time I wanted to push away."

Amelia reached across the table and took hold of my hand. Her caress against my skin said so much more than her words did. It was tender. Her thumb moving against mine was a seductive dance that felt like she understood this deeper connection we'd been dancing around.

"That's great news!" Henry clapped his hand against his other before saying, "I'm really impressed with your work so far. Keep up the good work! How about the rest of you? Who wants to update us next?"

Once the round robin completed, Elyse came back with the laser focus on Amelia.

"I wanted to give you the opportunity, knowing that this is a support group, to share—however you see fit—what happened with you at the V.A. You mentioned you were glad to have your care coordinator help you. I want you to know that this is a support group for any hurdle you're overcoming. In case there are ways you feel we could encourage your growth."

Honestly, I wanted to know what went on as well. I figured she would share those things at some point with me privately and not leave me hanging. We locked eyes, and I felt her gaze all the way down my spinal cord. It was as if the weirdness of last Sunday had been totally forgotten.

"I think that the people who can best support me already are helping me through the situation."

The way she blushed when she looked my way. I felt myself hardening all over again. I silently cursed Elyse for her focused attention, as Amelia had taken her hand away and put it back in her lap.

"Just tell me how," I whispered, caught up in the remembrances of our heated exchange. "Any support I can give."

I must have said it too loudly because the whole room stared at the two of us.

"Why would Emmett get to know and not the rest of us?" One of the other amps, a woman by the name of Nancy, asked. "I feel like this group is about building trust and supporting one another while we all try to figure life out. The good and the bad. So wouldn't you want to share with all of us?"

The group started to chatter amongst themselves, the volume in the room rising to a level that started to put me on edge. The women started talking amongst themselves wondering why Amelia would take me into her confidences but not share with them. One of them—it sounded like Nancy, but I couldn't be certain—told one of the other people at the table that Amelia had always been a standoffish *bitch*. Hearing them disparaging her was the equivalent of picking up a light and setting a fuse burning.

"We're dating! That's why! And it pertains to me. We were making out and she had a panic attack. Okay? Are you happy now?"

I can say most assuredly one person who wasn't happy. Amelia.

"That was my personal, private business that you decided to share without permission."

After loose lips Emmett shouted the private details of my life at the top of his lungs, Henry escorted us out of the ballroom. Emmett sat in a wingback chair, eyes full of pleading entreaty, trying to grab my hand each time I passed in front of him. I couldn't sit as Henry had asked me to at least four times. My whole body felt like I'd kicked over a hornet's nest and they all buzzed desperate to find a place to land and strike.

"Amelia, I realize that you may not be thrilled that Emmett shared the fact that the two of you are dating with everyone, but I want to make you aware that your reaction to this problem lends to the same behavior pattern as when you are resisting. Is it possible that Emmett wasn't intentionally or maliciously sharing that news?"

Emmett reached for my hand, and as desperately I wanted to pull it away. I didn't want Henry to say that was another gesture that signaled I was resistant to anything other than showing Emmett my obvious displeasure. That was until he placed a kiss on my hand. His lips on my skin created a butterfly effect of tenderness that radiated through my whole bloodstream.

"I ove reacted," he began. The skin around his eyes crinkled, his downturned lips hinting at the concern he professed. "People were whispering, and I could hear the judgment in their voices. I just," he sighed, flexing his fingers against mine a second time, "they have no right to stand in judgment of you. Everyone started speaking at once and it got so loud and out of control in there. I just needed them all to shut up and stop being so nosey."

He pulled on my arm, and I didn't resist. I stood in front of him, allowing him to guide me between his legs. My hands went to his face of their own accord, framing his pouty mouth and puppy dog eyes between my hands.

"People are always going to judge us, right? Last week it was the kids at the fair calling us freaks this week Nancy thinks I'm a cold bitch. If anyone should be fighting against them and trying to convince them I'm not—it's me, the resister." I laughed, a lightbulb going off in my head just as the words came out of my mouth "I know you just want to protect me, but this is our reality. Moving through life as less than whole in the eyes of the world."

He turned his face, placing a tender kiss to the inside of my wrist, and the contact felt like it zipped through every vein in my entire body.

"You have enough pain you're trying to sort through." His voice was low, quieter than a whisper. "If I can protect you from having to experience additional pain from a couple of assholes, I can't promise I won't do it again."

"I'm really proud of both of you." Henry slapped his thighs, breaking the sweet moment. "Not only on the work that you're doing, but the obvious respect you treat one another with."

He stood up, and I thought he was going to go back inside, but he turned and faced us again, leaning against the back of the chair.

"Emmett, given that you tend to just roll with whatever happens, you taking control of that situation and advocating for the two of you—it shows that you've really been thinking about our lessons here and how to apply them."

Before he went back into the banquet hall, he turned one last time. "I think the two of you will be a great couple. You're just different enough that you're a compliment to one another.'

Support group finished without incident. I followed Emmett back to the tavern in the sweet SUV the rental company put me in while my little Hyundai was being fixed. Driving it all week had me wondering if it was time to get a car that was made to accommodate my new reality, instead of continuing to squish myself into a tiny car that I'd had since before the accident.

"I brought a bag." The heat on my face could probably be

used to cook the entirety of their holiday spread. "I hoped you might not mind having a house guest."

It was so forward of me. I wasn't typically that girl. After speaking with my doctors, however, I hadn't been able to stop thinking about trying again with Emmett.

"I thought maybe we could make a second attempt at last weekend."

The moment the words were out of my mouth I remembered that the last time I was here Finn cleaned my stuff out for me and brought it back to the restaurant. I'd stayed with Finn and Gemini until the bridge opened back up the following afternoon. That wasn't the memory I wanted to surface in my head or in his.

"We could skip the party and I can show you what an accommodating host I can be?"

He wriggled his eyebrows at me and wrapped his arm around my back. His face was close enough that I could smell the peppermint bark Gemini had insisted everyone finish before the meeting concluded. It was the first time I was this close to him not under the influence of alcohol or hormones. There was the teeniest scar just below his eyebrow and I wondered if that was a result of the rail yard accident or him being a wreckless kid. Knowing how far back his friendship went with Finn, I could picture the two of them running around in the woods surrounding The Tavern, creating secret hideaways up in the trees or between the rock formations.

"I was really excited to come today. I didn't know how I'd feel after last weekend," I told him, relishing in the feel of being held by him. "Even with someone's big mouth in group," I raise my eyebrow at him and pin him with a look of displeasure, "just seeing you sitting at the table with a seat saved for me, made me kinda giddy."

He took hold of my braid, pulling my head back gently so I could look him in the eye, and softly said, "Kiss me."

I tilted my head up to meet him halfway. It was definitely not just a kiss, however. He made a topographical exploration of every ridge and sensitive spot along the seam of my lips before parting them with his tongue and doing the same to my top and bottom lip alone.

"We have a couple hours before we have to get ready. We can talk about what happened at the V.A."

He extended his hand, wiggling his fingers until I took it, and I followed him into the restaurant. With the exception of some staff setting up for the party, and Finn bustling around the kitchen, the restaurant was empty. He led me to the booth in the back I'd sat at the last time I was here. A server saw that we'd taken a seat and rushed over with a bottle of water and basket of fresh made chips that they provided to the tables.

"I have residual nerve damage," I told him, just deciding that a direct route was the best course of action. "The nerve that my doctors and I talked about, the peroneal nerve, not only lives in the leg and the upper thigh, but also extends into the sex organs. So, when we were making out last weekend, all of a sudden that nerve got hyper stimulated. My body didn't know how to process all of it and reacted by overcompensating and rushing too many signals through my body. Since many of the nerves it tried to send signals to are either dead from the amputation, or are trying to grow back, a lot of those signals had nowhere to go so they just hang out at the furthest place the signal traveled and kind of accumulate. The pain was really intense. So intense, in fact, that it triggered me back to being in Afghanistan. And that's why I started screaming."

"I'm so sorry, Amelia." He reached across the booth and gathered my hands in his. "I can't even imagine not only the pain but how scary that must have been. After I acted like an ass a few hours ago, I really am honored you trusted me with that information. I had no idea that this is what you were going through."

"Henry was right," I began. "Part of my resistance is in allowing people to see me in vulnerable situations. Some of that comes from my military training, but it also comes from being in a family of immigrants, who were really poor and looked down upon. That dependency on others led to a lot of negative feelings towards others."

There was more sitting on the tip of my tongue waiting to be spoken if I could find the nerve to say it. My phone chimed with an incoming text, interrupting our conversation. Normally, I'd ignore a text from anyone if I was in the middle of a conversation, but Staff Sergeant Jones had a special ring tone that only he had. Specifically, so that I knew if he called or texted, I would be aware of it any time I was able to answer.

> Jones: Just me, asking again to please consider coming.

"Who's that?" Emmett asked, playfully trying to sneak a peek at my phone.

"It's my old C.O.," I explained as I typed a reply. "He's getting married in a few weeks and has been trying to get me to agree to go to New York for the wedding."

"Why wouldn't you?" Emmett asked.

"It's complicated. Really complicated."

"So, tell me. Maybe I can help you uncomplicate it."

With a sigh I set my phone down.

"There's way too many pieces to be able to accurately

uncomplicate things in the limited time we have before the party starts."

"Amelia." It was the first time I'd seen him look stern. Not a playful stern either. "Just because Henry said we did a good job, doesn't mean I can't still 'check' you."

His attempt at stern lasted all of four seconds before melting into the flirty smile he usually wore. Seeing it reappear sent a giddy sensation all the way through my nervous system.

"I don't want everyone staring at me." Maybe if I went that route he'd absolve me from having to say the rest.

"People stare at you all the time, it's never bugged you before."

"Yes, but I wasn't walking into someone's wedding when they did. All eyes should be on the bride and groom, not on the circus act."

Being stared at was only half that concern. Did I wear a long dress so no one could see my leg, but risk tripping over it at some point during the night. Or did I wear a short dress, avoid tripping hazards but really draw all eyes to me as I walked around his reception.

"I'm assuming that if he's inviting you, you must have a pretty decent friendship?"

I nodded, accepting a glass of wine from our server, who also set down a charcuterie board for us to snack on.

"If it weren't for him, I don't think I'd be alive. I definitely wouldn't have had access to the kind of care I've received, and certainly wouldn't have been sent to Germany so quickly."

I shook my head as if just that act alone would keep the rush of images at bay. I begged my subconscious to keep me in the moment, talking to Emmett, enjoying the wine, and chatting and getting to know one another. I fought against the onslaught of memories from Afghanistan with every ounce of my being, focusing instead on the way it felt to have Emmett's lips on mine, and how comforting it was when he wrapped his arm around my back.

"Hey," I jolted at Emmett's touch, "come back."

His voice was as soft as his touch had been. The perfect pull back to actual reality. I opened my eyes and saw him sitting there, his compassionate eyes making a study of my face. He brought me back. I'd teetered on the edge, and he'd been my talisman.

"I think you should go. Actually, no thinking about it. Just do it. Book the plane ticket and go. Period. If he means that much to you and had that big of a hand in making sure you were okay, then you should be there for his big day."

I huffed into my wine glass. In my head, all of the reasons why I shouldn't go flew to the front of my brain demanding they be taken into consideration. Just thinking of those reasons sent a tremble down my spine.

"Emmett, there's a lot of baggage tied to my attending that wedding. The last thing I want to do is be a distraction on Jones's big day. Me being there would be a gigantic distraction. And not just because of my leg."

"Whatever it is, Amelia, I'm certain none of it could overshadow the fact that this Jones guy is getting married. Everyone attending surely wants to be present for that."

"Emmett, you don't understand."

I could feel my throat tightening. Felt the tickle in my throat as my lungs tried to protect themselves from all of the smoke. Hear Garcia crying out, praying in Spanish. I didn't hear anything from the guys in the back—Dan, who they called Sunshine, and Ivan, who they called Terrible. They'd died instantly, I'd found out later. They weren't even in the Humvee anymore. The sheer power of that blast propelled them almost a full football field into the desert.

"Amelia," his soft voice again, "stay with me."

"Men died, Emmett. Good men. Men I barely knew because I'd just barely been assigned to Tenth Mountain eight weeks before that. I was a total newb. Their friends, who were on their second tour, all died, but I lived. Those guys going to Jonesy's wedding, Bishop and Ram, Diesel, Hollywood, the whole unit—I'm a reminder of one of the most painful days for that unit. I promise you they don't want to see me."

Rather than say anything, he came around and sat next to me on my side of the booth. He wrapped his arm around my back and pulled me against his chest, tucking me under his chin. I melted into his hug. Every muscle in my body sighed feeling the strength of his chest and the surety of that embrace. I wanted that feeling more. To be surrounded by it. Every emotion that whispered in my psyche while held in his embrace: safety, comfort, compassion, and rapidly developing feelings of tenderness and—other words that I didn't want to give voice to—I realized how badly I needed them. Craved them even. They were all the emotions that I'd been trained to suppress. Things I pushed down into the darkest crevices of my personality so as not to be perceived as weak or incapable. But I did need them, and Emmett was beyond exceptional at providing them.

CHAPTER SIXTEEN

With the holiday party about to start, I didn't want to push the subject. She needed to go to that wedding though. I was no Henry "Coping is Moping" Jennings, I could see that Amelia's pattern of resisting extended even into her military life. While she may have been hesitant to see all those guys out of fear they'd somehow blame her for their friends being gone, I think a few years down the road she might regret not attending.

"Amelia said she'll be ready in ten minutes." Gemini breezed by me in the kitchen, where I had begun plating our first course.

"Say, Gem." I looked up to see her frying pork belly in a cast iron skillet for our main course. "On a scale of one to ten how much do you like dress shopping?"

"I'd say a mini would probably look best on you... a ballgown would be a fire hazard around all of this open flame." She threw her head back and cackled at her own joke, shaking the pan before starting a roue in a second pan.

"You should really take your comedy tour on the road. Seriously, though. Amelia got invited to her commander's wedding. I think one of the reasons she doesn't want to go is because she's embarrassed about her leg. I thought maybe if you took her to whatever place has fancy dresses, and maybe helped her try some on—you know, grab them for her while she stands in the dressing room—maybe she'd change her mind."

Gemini had been a flurry of activity organizing all of her pans for the main course. She stopped everything she was doing to turn and look at me. With her hands on her hips, she cocked her head, a full, toothy smile on her face.

"Aww Emmett's sweet on Amelia." She made a few obnoxious kissing noises before turning back to her sizzling pans.

"You're such a child, Gem." I tossed a dish towel at the back of her head. "I'm being serious though. Do you think you could invite her out shopping? Maybe have some fake event you need to go to and ask her help deciding on a dress. Or, you know, however you think you could get her to agree to go."

"Did she say she was going to go to the wedding?"

"No, not yet." I shrugged. "I'm hoping I can convince her to go. I just ... I know she'll regret it if she doesn't go."

"Most of the crowd's been fed," Finn handed me a plate. "Why not take this to your woman. Go enjoy dinner with her."

Amelia sat in the same booth I'd put her in earlier. She'd styled her hair down, her curly-cue hair had been flattened into soft round curls. I wanted to reach out and twist them around my finger, to feel their silkiness and test their bounce.

"That smells divine!"

She clapped softly as I set the plate down in front of her. Finn came in right behind me to drop off a plate for me and left a bottle of wine.

"You are such an inspiration, Emmett." She beamed at me with a full toothy smile. "A self-taught chef. It's not something you see every day."

"Well, I'm not a chef. I just like to cook. Gemini is the chef. For the most part I do what she tells me to do." I took a sip of the wine Finn brought to the table, reflecting on the past year. "I will say I've learned so much from Gemini."

"Oh! That's right. She told me once that I should ask you how you learned to cook."

She said it with such entertained glee that it was obvious she didn't know the pain attached to those memories.

"How did that conversation come up between you and Gemini?" I asked. "Out of curiosity. Because I can't imagine that Gemini would bring that up in a casual conversation."

The smile slid off her face faster than the last lap at a NASCAR race. I watched her fidget with her napkin, folding it over and over again across her lap. When she looked up at me again her face had tightened as if she was nervous to mention it.

"That first night I'd been at your house, and you made me go to Wal-Mart that next morning? Gem and I were in the car talking about her and Finn and what a good guy you were. And

I made a joke along the lines of how you must really love bulk shopping stores because everything in your house was in oversized containers."

She licked her lips, grabbing her water goblet and taking a long drink. I didn't want to interrupt her, but also didn't know if that was the extent of her explanation.

"Anyhow she said that Henry giving you 'adapt' as a verb was perfect for you because it's what you always did. And she mentioned that when you first lost your arm and were trying to find your way, the smaller jars and such at the grocery store were all twist jars, and being up here in hill country, there wasn't much access to accessible tools that would have helped you in the kitchen. Finn's dad owned the restaurant and gave you an industrial sized can opener—one of those electric ones, and so you just learned to adapt."

Wasn't Gemini the little songbird. While she'd given her some good history, she'd forgotten all of the important pieces. This wasn't the type of getting to know you chatter I wanted to have with Amelia. However, she had unloaded a whole lot of her trauma connected to her tour in Afghanistan, I guessed it was the least I could do.

"Gemini may have glossed over the key points," I started, twisting my fork over and again, playing with the few remaining bites of gratin in the ramekin. "The biggest being that hill people grow up poor. You know—you were mining poor; we were railyard poor. So we, too, depended on food banks and the like to fill in where the paycheck couldn't stretch. Food bank boxes tended to have a lot of random ingredients. Which meant from an early age I learned to at least make do with what we got. After I lost my arm, Pa wasn't ever much of a help and tended to ignore things that made me different. I just figured out ways around doing things. Like Gem said, Finn's dad was more of a help than my own pa. I used the tools that were available to me. If I bought an industrial size can of whole potatoes, I would find different ways to cook all of those potatoes until they were gone so that I didn't waste anything."

While I told Amelia my sad little tale, I made a study of her face. She had the most expressive eyes. I could guess which emotion she felt as I escorted her through my backstory just based on the twitch of an eyelid, the widening of her eyes, or the rounding of her eyelids.

"Have you ever thought about getting a prosthetic?"

"Not sure how a fake arm can help me any. Other than making me look better balanced."

"Oh, golly no. You'd be amazed what they've achieved in neuro-biotics. They can actually attach arms to nerves and tissue. You'd have basic functionality in some ways as if you never lost your arm."

I ran my arm against the back of my head, considering what she said.

"Truth is the rail yard gave me some money for injury. Said it was to help get me settled with a new arm and cover expenses and whatnot. But it barely covered the hospital bills. By the time we paid off the emergency room and the surgeon, I had just enough to go to community college and buy into Finn's bar. And now it's been so long, I don't think it would ever be a possibility even if I wanted to."

"Well, if you ever decide you want to at least talk to a doctor...I can put you in touch with mine."

There was a local band playing songs quietly in the corner of the room. As people finished their main courses and waited for dessert to be plated, a few meandered up to where the band circled around the Christmas tree and started dancing.

"Will you do me a big favor?" I asked, just as the band switched into "Have Yourself a Merry Little Christmas."

"What?" She looked at me, then blushed and lowered her

eyelids, so I could only see the metallic swipe of eyeshadow on her lids and her lush eyelashes.

I stood, taking a deep breath, steeling myself for her rejection. Silently I begged her to be open to my suggestion. I extended my hand to her with a smile before asking, "Dance with me?"

The rejection formed on her lips, furrowing her brow, milliseconds after I asked her.

"We don't have to go up there." I nodded towards the stage. "You've shared so much with me today, and I just really want to feel you close while I still have to finish up the party. Just one song?"

I watched her bite her lip while she considered it. She turned and stole a glance at the makeshift stage before turning back towards me. With a resigned sigh, she put her napkin on the table and began scooting, accepting my hand to help her up.

"When I was a little kid," I whispered, her cheek resting against mine while we slowly danced right in front of the booth we'd occupied, "I used to wonder if my mom and dad ever danced like they did on TV shows. They obviously had to have feelings for one another to get married and make me."

Amelia pulled her head away from my cheek to look me in the eyes, and chuckled when I wiggled my eyebrows at her.

"But I never saw my dad with anyone. My whole life he spent it alone. I like to think it was because he was so in love with my mom that losing her hurt as much as losing a piece of himself."

"He never talked about her?" Amelia asked, running her hand along my jaw. I just shook my head. I couldn't explain the complexity that was my pa without ruining the magic bubble that surrounded us.

"My parents can't keep their hands off each other." She laughed. "If the eight kids weren't evident enough, they take every opportunity to kiss, canoodle, make out—however you want to frame it. Even now. At nearly seventy. There has never been a day in my life that I ever doubted how much they loved one another and *all* of us."

"I guess you could say despite being hill poor you were rich with love."

She looked up at me, and the emotion I saw in her eyes made me nearly lose my step and trip us both. I must have had way too much wine, because the look in her eyes felt too tender to be a passing interest in me. That maybe she actually did want to date me, potentially even love me someday.

CHAPTER SEVENTEEN

Amelia

The night was pure magic. Delicious food aside, I loved learning more about Emmett and what made him tick. How ironic, also, that our two worlds orbited close enough to one another that over the years we could have passed by one another at a store, or in a movie theater, and who knows maybe the whole trajectory of our lives would have changed.

"Did I tell you how beautiful you look tonight?" Emmett pushed the handbrake on his truck, looking over at me as the inside lights of his truck began to brighten.

"You didn't," I replied. "But I'll accept a late compliment just the same."

I'd been brave and daring and wore bootcut jeans instead of my usual yoga pants. Despite being in a fairly simple sweater, I pulled out the fancy lingerie just in case when Emmett and I finished dinner I had a desire to see where the evening took us. For the first time in years, I felt sexy and desired, and I wanted to keep that feeling going for as long as I could.

"So, what do you want to do now?" He turned toward me from the driver seat, pushing the button that undid his seatbelt for him.

"I can think of a few things."

My lack of experience had created a discomfort in my own body and sexuality long before I'd lost my leg. That only compounded my feelings. But spending the time with Emmett, knowing that he found me attractive and wanted to explore where this relationship went as much as I did, made me feel bold. Confident. Like I could ask that my needs be met and feel totally safe in doing so.

I practically floated from his truck to the guest bedroom. He had my bag in his hand, which he set on top of the dresser. The scene felt familiar, yet the air felt heavy with the promise of how different it would be. I pulled my sweater over my head, surprised at how badly I wanted him to appreciate the red satin bra I wore beneath.

"Ms. Sanchez, I approve on so many levels."

He reached his hand out, and then thought better of it, tucking it into his pocket.

"I'm a little nervous," a bubble of anxiety disguised as a

giggle erupted from between my lips, "I don't know where the line is. You know between feeling good and falling into a flashback." I took his hand and placed it over my breast. "I'm hoping that if I tell my body what's going to happen ahead of time, then maybe my brain will know where to direct all of that sensation."

He caressed my breast, running his palm along the satin. His fingers tickled along the skin just beneath the fabric, and the first wave of pleasure skittered through my system. I braced for a shock of pain that never came.

"If all we do is this—"

"Shh," I kissed away his statement, "let's just look for the line together."

"Why don't you lie down?" he suggested. "Trying to stay balanced while getting woozy on pleasure might be too much for your body to try to do at once."

I lowered myself onto the bed, looking up at him in anticipation.

"Button?" he asked, pointing at my jeans.

I'd completely forgotten he didn't have two hands to manipulate a button. Once I freed the button and zipper, Emmett guided them off my hips. His fingers traced the skin of my fully functioning thigh, the tickle forcing my eyes closed and turning my muscles to jelly. He followed his fingers with his lips. Tracing up my thigh, over my hip bone, across the muscles of my stomach. They twitched as his lips traveled across them, causing him to stop.

"Are you okay?"

I was lost in a haze of delicious sensation. It took me a moment to realize he'd asked me a question. So far, every touch from Emmett on my body had been a welcome experience. My mouth had gone dry, and it took me a moment to re-introduce any moisture back onto my lips.

"I've read in a few books that sometimes people use colors. You know, so you don't have to keep asking if everything is okay. Green means go, yellow means slow down, red means stop," I suggested.

"How about anything that feels remotely not good, you call red. I would rather stop before you tip over into agony."

"Deal." I smiled at him, drawing patterns on my stomach, hoping to keep my body hanging in that hyperaware state of pleasure I'd just been dancing with.

"Would you like to keep your leg on?"

That's right. My leg. I sat up and pressed the release button, immediately moaning at how good it felt to take my leg out and give it some freedom for the rest of the night.

Emmett's hand joined mine, mimicking how I rubbed the muscles to help them relax.

"Roll onto your stomach," Emmett suggested.

Though there was a bit of hesitation on my part, I did as he asked. As soon as I settled into a comfortable position, his hand rested against my haunch. He worked the muscles around my hip and upper thigh with such focus and gentle but firm touch that I was moaning and writhing like an eel.

"Puzzle pieces," he said, running his hand up and down along the muscle that always tightened up on me. "Where you lack, I'm strong. And where I lack, you are strong."

I realized that with me on my stomach, his functioning arm was better able to get a grip on the area above my missing leg. From the front he had to cross his arm over his body to access it.

I heard him slip out of his shirt, the fabric sighing as it went over his head and onto the floor. Followed by the tinkling of a belt buckle and the thunk of his pants hitting the floor.

"Still green?" he asked, running his hand up and down the muscles of my back. "I wish I had both my hands right now, angel. You deserve to feel consumed by bliss, instead of having it stop and start in fits."

He leaned over me, lips at my neck, tracing the dip of the muscles along my shoulder. I felt his cock hot and hard against my panties. With every movement, Emmett made to situate himself and keep balance while teasing my neck and back, his cock further ingratiated itself between my cheeks.

"You okay?" He pushed off the bed, leaning back and away from my body.

"Mmm, I'm more than okay, Emmett."

"You didn't answer me when I asked." He ran his hand down my back to caress my ass. "I was worried."

"I need to shift positions," I told him. "Can you help me up to the pillows?"

I tried not to feel shame or embarrassment. But my tolerance for positions where a joint or limb was working against gravity, put pressure on my whole body, and a halo of pain began to circle. I wanted to make sure to cut it off before it had the chance to surface.

Having situated myself on the pillows, I had full visual access to Emmett's body. I don't know what I expected to see when looking at where his arm should be, but I hadn't been prepared for the violence of his scar tissue. Even the worst of us that lost limbs overseas were tended to by highly trained surgeons, so the scars that we bore were much cleaner and less apparent. Emmett's scar looked as if he'd fought a bear and lived to tell the story. I fought against the well of tears I could feel fighting to be spilled.

"Kiss me," I whispered. "Please kiss me."

I poured everything into that kiss. All of the pain I felt for him, knowing he'd suffered through such a traumatic event alone, and with no access to the kinds of resources I did.

"It happened a long time ago, Amelia," he told me, running his lips along my forehead. "It doesn't hurt me anymore."

It hurt me though. It hurt me knowing that a young man went to work one day and his whole world changed. And, while his world changed, he had to face that new frontier totally alone.

CHAPTER EIGHTEEN

I couldn't bear to see that look in her eyes. It wasn't pity. Pity I'd become accustomed to. Pity I could write off, close my eyes against, and ignore. Amelia's eyes overflowed with empathy and compassion. They felt too warm. Held my insides together in a way that I'd not even realized I wanted to be touched. Those feelings were too much to think about or be too close too. Thankfully, before I had time to spin further into my own head, she lifted off the pillows, reached behind her and unclipped her bra, revealing a tantalizing pair of teardrop breasts.

"Oh, Amelia. You're too beautiful, angel. So, so beautiful."

My mouth watered in desperation to take greedy pulls from her stiff peaks. To run my thumb along one hard nub, enjoying how much she writhed and moaned while I did. But, rather than dive in, something held me back.

Gently, I ran my tongue from her collarbone, down her clavicle, and around the upswell of her breast.

"Green?" I asked.

"Very green." She smiled, sighing as she adjusted herself against the pillow. Her fingernails played along my hairline, massaging my scalp and tickling the sensitive skin of my neck. With the green light, I took a nipple into my mouth, rolling around my tongue. She moaned and held my head in place, her hips gyrating of their own accord with each gentle pull against one of her turgid peaks.

"Oh gosh, Emmett. It's so good."

I wondered offhand the last time she'd gotten off. Had she touched herself at all since coming home? Or did all of this nerve damage she talked about with her doctor, detract her from self-exploration.

"I want to try something," I told her, leaning back against my legs. "The first sign of any kind of discomfort, you tell me okay?"

She nodded, biting her lip. Her breath came in rapid pulls that made her breasts sway in the most tantalizing way. I wanted to dive back in for a second helping, but I needed to know just how far out the line between pleasure and pain was.

"I'm going to put my lips lower. If it gets too intense, tell me."

"Okay," she told me on a sigh. Beneath me her thighs relaxed, opening far enough to provide me space to move between them. The satin panties that she'd worn for me broadcast just how much her body enjoyed every minute of what we'd done so far.

I took her functioning thigh in my hand, resting it on my shoulder. I traced patterns along the skin of her thigh, thoroughly enjoying when her ass launched off the bed as pleasure erupted into her body.

"Still green, angel, or are you yellow?"

Her thigh muscle still felt lax in my hand. There was no tension in it at all, which told me she had to still be enjoying it. She sighed my name and told me green seconds later.

I turned and focused my attention on the other thigh, sticking to the inside, closest to her panty line and staying clear away from the scar tissue. I suckled and nibbled the fleshy part of her inner thigh, getting drunk both on the way she moaned and writhed but also from the scent of her increasing arousal. With no color being announced, and a green from Amelia when I asked her, I explored her satin covered mound. She didn't appear to have any sensation along her little nub. I ran my nose along her seam, teased it over her panties with my tongue, and there appeared to be no response. Though running my fingers along the inside of her thighs, especially the uninjured one, had her practically orgasmic.

"I want to feel your pussy, angel. Do you have any pain before I touch it?"

She looked me in the eye, a shy smile on her lips, and shook her head in the negative.

I ran my nails up along her lips, tickling into her well-trimmed mound, tracing along her seam.

"Emmett," she whispered, raising her hips up to meet me.

A pass of my fingertip against her clit yielded no reaction. I continued to explore, watching her face like an intensive study of the *Mona Lisa*. I looked for any clue to show me that she had any discomfort at all. I pressed into the warm depth of her pussy, and she clamped down on my fingers. It was so fast and so intense, I thought I'd hurt her, but a moment later, tongue between her teeth, she hissed out my name, fucking against those fingers. From within the walls of her entrance, I circled the inside in search of her g-spot. If her clit didn't have any feeling, I silently hoped her g-spot did. No matter how much I wiggled, pushed, or pulled I couldn't locate anything that hinted towards her secret little trigger. With each stretch of my fingers though, she keened and spread herself open for me.

"Does that feel good, angel?"

I balanced over her, running my nose along the bridge of her nose before kissing her. The moment our lips touched, a bonfire of lust sent my entire being into another stratosphere. Amelia wrapped her arms around my back, her nails drawing enticing patterns up and down my spine that had my whole circulatory system overloading on pleasure. I rubbed against her warm center, relishing in the sweet friction.

"Color, beautiful."

"Keep going." Her panted breath tickled against my lips. "I'm still good."

I was out of my briefs and sheathed in a nanosecond. My fingers teased beneath her panties one last time before they came off. With every pass through her desire, she'd beg for more. I tried desperately to keep a good, tight rein on my common sense. I wanted to explore Amelia's body over and over again. Therefore, I couldn't lose focus.

"Amelia, you still doing okay?" I lined my cock up against her pussy, gritting my teeth against the intense desire to push in.

"Yes, Emmett," she sighed, and I pushed home. Inch by slow inch.

I drowned in sensation. My whole being shifted in

awareness. Sounds were louder, sensations more intense, the room was awash in smells I hadn't even noticed, like the clean unassuming scent of Amelia's hair and soap, the subtle lavender scent of the sheets, and the cooking oil I could still smell on my skin.

I was already there. Six pumps and I could feel the tightness, the liquid heat inching its way up, begging for release. I made myself a string of promises that we'd do this more. Maybe even in a few hours if we could recover fast enough. I'd just convinced myself to let go because there was always next time when Amelia shouted, "Yellow! Emmet, please! Yellow. Yellow."

I pulled out, just as my orgasm broke free, shooting with such ferocity, my eyes and ears lost all access to stimuli for a brief moment, before the greasy tendrils of guilt stole away every last ounce of pleasure.

"Where does it hurt?" I tried to find my bearings. "Tell me, Amelia. Stay with me."

"Everywhere," she cried. "I feel like I'm on fire."

I tried to help her shift against my chest, her back to my front, and cradle her, hold her, whisper things in her ears. Anything to keep her in the here and now, and not slide into a full trigger.

"It's okay," I whispered, trying to hold her against me as much as I could. "It's okay."

AMELIA

"Don't leave me hanging here, Amelia. Then what happened?"

After the weekend with Emmett, I'd asked Pam if I could come and see her first thing Monday.

"I blacked out or passed out. I'm not sure what you would

call it. But one minute, I felt like every nerve ending in my body had rubbing alcohol poured on it, and the next I woke up and it was morning, and Emmet had slept behind me, holding me against his chest."

I'd been so embarrassed when I woke up, but god, Emmett was so apologetic and understanding. Larry and Jared Flynn had worked on my car all week and called on Saturday to tell me it was finished. Emmett followed me back to my house to drop off my Hyundai, and then I gave him a ride back to Barren Hill. We'd talked on the way home about what happened the night previous, and despite my objections he blamed himself for being too "lost in the moment" that he should have gone slower.

Pam took a sip of her coffee before placing it on her plug-in coffee warmer and making a note in my file. She flicked her pen between her finger and thumb, shaking it while she appeared to contemplate something in my file. The seconds hung between us while I watched her re-read what she wrote.

"This is progress," she began with a smile. "I think that perhaps you got a bit too excited over our meeting with the doctors last week. Given all of the obstacles in your way, it's possible you need to feel more emotional intimacy with Emmett."

"There was definitely attraction," I countered, confused as to why she would question the why of our hooking up.

"I don't doubt there's attraction. From the sound of it, he's both sweet and charming *and* easy on the eyes. However, you both have been through some significant trauma. While Emmett *appears* to be more accepting of his disability than you, it's possible he is battling with some feelings of inadequacy. Given his reaction every time something happens between you two. And, maybe you need to feel something deeper now that you have all of these damaged nerves.

Something else to give you the last lift over the hill to completion."

Not that I'd ever been a one night stand kind of girl, but prior to Afghanistan I certainly didn't need to feel emotionally connected in order to come.

"Trauma, Amelia," Pam replied as if reading my thoughts. "Your life is significantly different now than the last time you were physically intimate with anyone. Life changes us as much as our situations change. So perhaps the more trust you put into your relationship, the more satisfying the sex will be. It's purely a hypothesis, but one worth exploring."

I nodded, getting lost in my own thoughts. "I didn't get triggered back to Afghanistan," I told her, as if that alone was evidence of my trauma changing, "and the pain was intense. But intense in a different way. Sort of like pins and needles but they hurt at the same time. That's what it felt like—everywhere. As if my whole body had been asleep."

"Oh my god! Amelia, that could be really great news! I mean, not that you hurt, but this different feeling." She furiously jotted down more notes in my file. "We'll have to get you in with Dr. Xiao, but if you had an intense feeling of pins and needles—maybe, and I'm no expert so I can't say, but maybe that means your nervous system is trying to draw a new map?"

I hadn't thought about it that way. I'd been so embarrassed. And I felt so bad for Emmett. What a mess I was. How terrible that he's saddled with a woman whose body picks the absolute worst possible second to seize up and freak out.

"How did you leave things with Emmett?"

"God, he was so apologetic. I feel so bad."

"But you're still talking?"

I nod my head in place of answering, choosing instead to take another long sip of coffee.

"Well, unfortunately, Dr.Xiao doesn't have office hours today. She is usually here on Wednesdays, you know, the day you normally come in." She winked at me with feigned inconvenience. "I can get you on her schedule then?"

Jones: Just talked to your boyfriend. I'm so glad you changed your mind. Thank you for being willing to come celebrate my special day. It means so much to me. I know the rest of the unit will be thrilled to see you as well.

THE TEXT POPPED up as I was looking at my iCal to confirm I had availability. The name alone had me drawing in a breath, but the words? Took that breath right out of my lungs and refused to give it back.

"HEY, you okay? You went from smiling and laughing to a look of total panic. What's going on?"

I looked up at Pam and didn't even think I had access to words to explain the situation. He heard from *my boyfriend* I changed my mind? I was so confused. Where would he have even called that he came in contact with Emmett? Jones knew nothing about my life other than I was back at home at Haven's Cove and attending a support group in Barren Hill. It would take a lot of phone calls to even reach Emmett.

"Jones wants me to come to his wedding," I tell Pam.

"Oh that's great! I am so proud of you." She beamed as she made a note of it in my file. "That shows real growth, Amelia. Wow. I can't wait to report that up the chain. That support group of yours really is helping. When's the wedding?"

"New Year's Eve," I replied, still laser focused on my phone.

"I'll make a note in my file that you are approved to miss those support meetings." She reached across the desk and squeezed my hand. "Amelia, truly, I am floating on the pride I have for you. You really took what I said to heart and really jumped in with both feet. Seeing this kind of progress? It's days like this as a social worker that I live for."

With a reaction like that I couldn't tell her that I didn't want to go, that I was freaking out inside that he would even think I would. But she said she was proud of me. She was going to note in my file that I was healing and moving toward acceptance.

"I don't know if I can, Pam. Everyone will be there."

"And you will see that absolutely no one holds you accountable for an IED you would have no way of knowing was there. Seeing you will in no way detract from Jones's wedding. It will be great. Truly."

As I PULLED into The Tavern, an email came over from the airline, confirming my flight to New York. On a non-refundable flight. Jones bought me a non-refundable ticket. To his wedding, where I didn't even want to be.

"Hey! I thought I heard you pull up. Any interest in coming shopping with me? I'm just going to run to the bridal salon. It's so much easier than braving the mall. I'm headed to New York for New Year's, my friend Penn and his fiancé are moving to Chicago right after the first of the year, so they're throwing a big shindig and I need a fancy dress."

Gemini barely came up for air, as she met me in the parking lot.

"I don't know. I'm not really a frilly kind of person," I hedged. Plus, I wanted to get to the bottom of this magical plane ticket and wedding RSVP I had nothing to do with.

"Consider it a personal favor. I have no girlfriends here. And shopping by myself isn't nearly as fun. What about if I promise to keep it under thirty minutes?"

She smiled her charming smile and batted her eyelashes at me, repeating, "Please, please, please" under her breath.

"I would rather clean latrines than shop. Are you sure you want me to come with you?"

Gemini made a show of looking for other people in the parking lot.

"Seeing as how you're the only other woman I know who is remotely fun to hang out with, of course, I mean you. Thank you, thank you!" She practically squealed, opening my car door for me and holding my messenger bag while I got out of the car.

***

"I don't know how I feel about the green one. Is it too short? I feel like it's hitting me too high up on the thigh. Like if I bend over, everyone's getting a free show."

Gemini promised no more than thirty minutes and stuck to her word. She had four dresses picked out, two short, two long, within ten minutes of arriving at the store.

"Maybe I should give the long one a try again?"

"I like the one you have on. And I promise you, you can't see your rump. It's practically at your knee."

"Will you do me a huge favor?" she asked again.

"I think me being here was the huge favor."

"I know," she laughed, unzipping the dress. "Last favor. Can you put this on so I can see where it will come on me?"

"Gemini, we're two different sizes. And I have a Latina ass."

"And I have the ass of a chef that indulges in wine and pasta. So we're even stevens. Please... the dress. I won't ask for any more favors."

Gemini stepped out of it, right there in front of the mirror. She handed off the green sequined dress to me, pointing toward the room behind the curtain. She stood in her bra, with zero self-consciousness, not caring who saw her in her undies. Not that there was anyone else in the bridal store in the middle of the day on a Monday.

"What do you think?" she called out to me from outside the curtain.

The dress was actually pretty fierce. Even for me, with a messed-up leg, the sequin dress was just long enough that it hid the ugliest parts of my amputated leg, and was cut on a bias, which gave the illusion of an hourglass figure. The fabric stretched so even where it would have been tight over my thigh and prosthetic, it camouflaged all of the things I normally would be ashamed to have show.

"I think this is the perfect dress for you," I told her, pulling open the curtain. "It's not too short at all. In fact, it's the perfect length. And look at that, chef's ass, Latina ass—we really are similar!"

Gemini signaled to the salesperson that she was ready to pay. The sales clerk rang up the dress, which was on sale. That made Gemini even more happier and we were on our way back home within her promised thirty minutes.

"What kind of shoes do you think I need with that dress?"

"Well, I'm no help in that department." I pulled out my phone again, still totally befuddled as to how Jones thought I was going to his wedding.

"I haven't been able to wear heels in years."

"What would you wear then, since you can't wear heels?"

"Probably a sequined ballet flat."

The shoe conversation got cut short. The name "Jones" and his special ring tone lit up my phone.

"Now, I wonder why on earth you'd be calling me, two hours after you sent me a text message."

"Amelia, it is so good to hear your voice" Jones sounded relieved, actually. It was the first time I'd heard him sound more congenial than gruff. "And to hear such delight in it. You sound really happy, Sanchez. And there is no one I'd rather have all the happiness delivered to her feet than you."

"Well, I hope you'd wish that for your soon to be wife, as well, otherwise this could get a little awkward."

He laughed a loud belly laugh, drawing a giggle from me. Laughing like that was something that hadn't happened with enough frequency to remember the last time I had. It felt strange, but really good.

"Touché. Yes, her too. And speaking of significant others. A boyfriend for Amelia Sanchez? God, I am just speechless. It really set my mind at ease, knowing you've found peace and love, and you've grabbed hold of them. He sounds like he's a really great stand-up guy."

"What do you mean he sounds like a stand-up guy? I've never mentioned him to you before. I mean—it's still kind of new."

"I know. He told me when he called me this morning to tell me the good news about you coming to the wedding. He insisted that you didn't need any help paying for a ticket, but shit, Sanchez. I'm so damn excited to see you, I went ahead and bought one for you anyway. Emmett too. I just—can't wait to meet him and to catch up on what's been going on in your life lately."

Speechless. My mouth opened and closed, trying to form

words but nothing came out. My brain jumbled with too many converging thoughts.

"Listen, we're crazy here with wedding plans so I probably shouldn't hang on the phone for too long. But I'll see you in two weeks!"

With that the phone disconnected. I sat staring at it for what seemed like hours. But given the dress shop was less than fifteen minutes outside of town, it couldn't possibly have been that long. It wasn't long at all before we pulled up to The Tavern. Standing outside shooting the shit with the UPS guy was exactly the person I needed to talk to.

I watched Gemini pull up with Amelia in the passenger seat. Somehow Gemini had pulled it off. I wondered while I watched them chat in the front seat if Amelia even realized that the dress Gemini bought was for her. I prayed as I waved off the UPS driver that after some initial caterwauling she'd be excited to go to Jones's wedding.

"I'm just going to put this upstairs." Gemini winked at me as she practically skipped past, bringing the dress inside.

Amelia, rather than join Gemini on the path up to the restaurant, beelined for her car instead.

"Where ya going, angel?"

She ducked from my embrace. Her mouth twisted into the most intense frown I'd ever seen from her. Pissed was too light a word for how angry she looked.

"Hey. What's wrong?"

"Emmett, how could you? How did you? I'm so baffled right now."

She shucked off her messenger bag from her shoulder with such violence, the strap exited from her body with a violent *snap*. It sounded like it would have hurt, but her face gave no indication she even felt it before chucking it into the open door of her car and onto the passenger side.

"Let's go inside," I suggested, reaching for her hand. Rather than take it and follow me up the path, she twisted away from me, digging her heels right into the ground we stood on. She crossed her arms beneath her chest, noisily drawing in a deep breath.

"I don't want to go inside with you, Emmett. I want to know why. Why on earth would you meddle in my life? Especially with something that was none of your business, and I expressly said I had no interest in doing."

There was no opening in her monologue to interject, so I just stood there, waiting for her to finish. Hoping if she got it all out, she'd lose steam and maybe we could have a conversation. I tried once to get her to let me hug her, hoping if I could hold her, the rush of endorphins might calm her down.

"How on earth did this whole thing even happen?" she demanded, leaning against her car while she waited for an explanation.

"Saturday night, when you passed out, I got concerned."

We hadn't really talked about what happened after our

messy attempt at sex. At first I thought she'd just fallen asleep. But given what happened the time before at the Christmas tree lighting, I feared it was a black out.

"I thought maybe the overload of stimulus would do some damage to your brain, kind of like a concussion does. I mean, you had a little smile on your face, but who knows maybe that was a sign of a stroke or something. I got into my own head and started to really worry. Your phone was on the nightstand. Honestly at first, I was looking to see if you had your doctor stored in there. I was going to call and ask about blackouts. But I saw Jones's text message right at the top of your messages and thought he might know, since he would have experience with all kinds of soldiers. So I texted him and asked if he knew who your doctor was, that you'd had a moment of panic and blacked out and I wasn't sure if I needed to take you to the hospital. He told me that sleep was the body's way of resetting and that you would be fine and would wake up as if nothing happened."

She'd woken up smiling so I didn't think anything of it. I'd just been relieved that she didn't want to call Finn and have him play bodyguard while she collected her things and left again. But she stayed and we ate breakfast and had such a wonderful day that I didn't want to ruin it reflecting on what happened the night before.

"He called me this morning to check and see if everything was okay. We chatted for a bit, and he mentioned the wedding." I rolled my lips and tilted my head back towards the sky, as if the answer to my question would drop from the clouds, "Look Amelia, if you don't go, you'll regret it. You will. If the esteem you hold Jones in for all he did with you truly means as much as you say it does, then one day you'll look back and wish you hadn't been too afraid to attend."

"Afraid?" She looked at me as if I'd just told her the earth was flat. "You have absolutely no idea what it's like, Emmett."

"So tell me. Please." If I had two hands, they would have both held out in front of me, as if truly begging. She kept so many things close to the vest and I desperately wanted to know where her head was at. "What is holding you back from seeing your friend? For being happy for him. Enjoying his party and reconnecting with your old unit? Don't be resistant to new experiences Amelia, just because you've convinced yourself that they're all upset with you."

"How dare you!" she shouted, pointing at me with such ferocity, I nearly thought her finger would detach and turn into a missile landing right in my eye. "Me being there with this broken body will only remind every man of the 10th about things they want to forget. Imagine what it would be like seeing twelve men, and having them all have an attack like me, but all at the same time and in the middle of a wedding ceremony for someone you respect the hell out of. What kind of wedding memories would those be? As a bride, would you really want to think back on your special day and remember the moment the handicapped chick walked into St. Augustine's and triggered a pew full of soldiers?"

She went from angry enough to spit nails, to quiet and off balance.

"Amelia? Talk to me. What's happening?"

Dread choked off any more words. Her body folded onto the pavement. My reflexes weren't quick enough to catch her totally, but enough to gentle her fall as I yelled for Gemini and Finn to come and help.

CHAPTER TWENTY

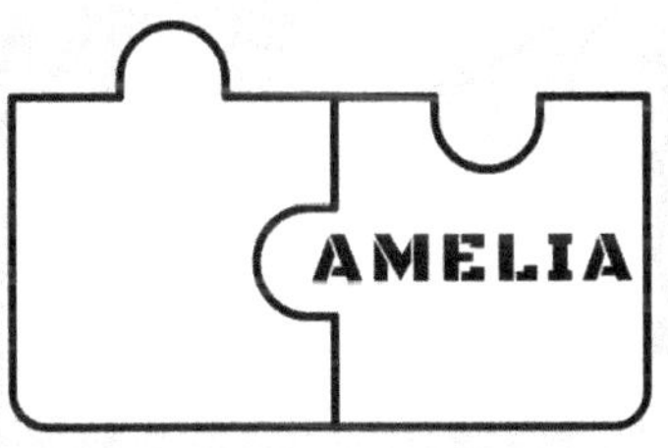

The last thing I remembered happening was Emmett and I arguing in the parking lot about going to Jones' wedding. We were talking about my friends from the 10th, and my consciousness flooded with a rapid flash of all of their faces in my head. I never got to say goodbye to any of them. Never got to tell them what happened. How I held Garcia and told him help was coming. Promised to deliver messages to his wife and kids, begged him to hold on. How happy we had all been just seconds before it happened. That Dan was singing stupid Christmasy songs to Ivan in the backseat, making up his own words to "Favorite Things."

I never heard from any of them other than Jones. Not Ridge, or Wolf, or even Diesel, who had always been like a big brother to me. I knew why. I was a reminder. I was a billboard to the fragility of life and how we could do everything right, thinking we'd traveled the same road a hundred times without incident, and something completely out of our control changed the trajectory of our life's journey forever. Talking to me while still in a battle zone meant coming face to face with the reminder that it could have been them.

"Silver lining to these blackouts, we can at least find a kernel of a pattern, right?" My neurologist, whose name I learned was Dr. Feinberg, detailed what we knew. "It seems that when your body takes in too much stimuli at once, whether positive or negative, your system overloads. This is a good thing, though the blackouts are really scary, I know. It means that your nervous system is trying to remap itself. A lot of these roads within your body, called neural pathways, are on express trains from your brain to the part of your body where the stimulus originated. When it finds a roadblock, it joins up with another train and hitches a ride and the two of them try to find a road. If those two get blocked, they hitch with another and so on, which means you have a freight train of sensation ping ponging throughout your body trying to find an outlet for all of that stimulus.

"Now let's say that freight train of stimulus finds a new bridge—a rebuilt neural pathway—and takes that bridge which was just built and is still very sensitive, and crosses it at full speed, with a hundred cars attached to it. That's what creates the blackout."

I nodded as if I heard him, but really, my mind was still on the conversation I had with Emmett the day before.

"It's no one's fault, Emmet," I'd told him. *"I shouldn't have attended a civilian support group. There's just too much baggage that you don't understand."*

I was barely able to look him in his eyes. He looked shattered. But it didn't make sense to continue to try to push forward with someone who could make such a one-sided decision about something so huge and think I'd be happy with that surprise.

"You're resisting, Amelia," he'd told me.

"No Emmett, you're trying to force me into your coping strategy. Not everyone can just shrug their shoulders and roll with the punches. Not everyone's life is as simple as a small mountain town and a local tavern. Afghanistan changed me, Emmett, and not in a good way. But it's not fair to you for me to make you adapt to the chaos. And that's what you'd do. Because it's who you are. You'd figure out how to make it okay, and suddenly your life would be chaos too."

"This whole thing, your speech, pushing me away, tapping out when you get scared—it's all resistance, Amelia. You are falling right into your old coping method. Pam, your team, Jones, they're all going to be so disappointed that when the going got tough, you turned tail and ran."

"Earth to Amelia," Pam patted my hand. "Did you hear what Dr. Xiao asked you?"

I shook my head, really to try to force myself back into the present, but Dr. Xiao took it as a shake in the negative to hearing her question and repeated it.

"When you and Emmett engaged in intercourse, you said that there were moments of pleasure right? That you were enjoying yourself? No pain? No flashback?"

My face tickled, and for a moment, I worried that I had

somehow triggered some kind of event that would have me blacking out again. But, when a wet droplet plopped onto my hand, where it rested in my lap I realized I was crying. And not just a single tear, but the realization of the one droplet brought on a waterfall of them.

"It was magic, Dr. Xiao. I felt sensation everywhere. In the best way."

Before I could describe my entire sexual experience with the flowery phrasing of a romance novel, she cut in with a follow up question. "With the exception of the sex organs, correct? Lack of sensation in the clitoris. What about the g-spot?"

"I honestly don't remember. I wasn't thinking in a clinical way. I was in the moment, grateful to have been able to stay present and enjoy being with him."

I couldn't say his name. Thinking about it hurt. That just Saturday everything was great, and today I sat in a doctor's office, dissecting my sex life that I would no longer had because I pushed him away.

"I think that maybe try again on a night where you haven't had any alcohol. That constricts blood vessels and may be the cause of some of the problem. Grab a couple toys from your preferred shop, whether that's online or in person, and just explore. Don't make the orgasm the destination. As you establish a connection, and that connection deepens, I suspect that eventually as you heal physically, and psychologically allow yourself the freedom of exploration, you'll find a fully satisfying sexual experience."

Once again, she handed me a pamphlet. This one was for couples and promised to aid in asking for what we needed to find sexual fulfillment. Unfortunately, given I just told Emmett that we should go our separate ways, it would be a while before I'd be fulfilled in any way.

CHAPTER TWENTY-ONE

Distracted didn't even sum up with accuracy how I felt. It was as if my brain were cable television, and my emotions couldn't settle on a channel. I'd pick up my phone to call Amelia, to see if she had a moment to calm down and examine the situation logically and talked myself out of it.

She was right, I didn't understand what it was like to be a soldier. I had no idea what she went through. I couldn't fathom the strain it puts on someone psychologically to watch your best friend die. But that didn't mean that I didn't want to be there to support her. To hold her when she was scared. To shoulder some of that burden that she carried alone.

"Henry," I asked. "How do I know the difference between coping and care? If you say my coping strategy is adapt, but life in general requires you to adapt to various situations, how do I know when I'm doing it for good and when I'm doing it wrong? Because right now I feel like I've failed at everything you've tried to teach us."

Amelia didn't show up for group. Everyone noticed her absence. Though no one said anything to me directly, I could feel them all staring at me. I could sense the judgment in those looks, silently blaming me. They could stare at me all they wanted. I didn't care. My concern was Amelia and whether she'd get in trouble for not attending her required meeting, all to avoid seeing me. I should have stayed home. Told Gemini to tell her that the meeting was hers.

"Why don't you tell me what the situation is? It's hard to be able to give you a clear delineation without knowing the situation."

Everyone around the table perked up. Nosey assholes. I rolled my eyes and dove into our fight. I left out the sex and all of the parts of our story from Saturday night that were wonderful but ours alone.

"Let me get this straight," Nancy spoke up first, "you went behind her back, called her C.O. and RSVP'd for a wedding she explicitly told you she didn't want to attend?"

I nodded. I couldn't look her in the eyes. I already knew what her face would look like. The same way Gemini's had, the same way everyone else whom I'd told looked at me. Like I'd been crazy and overstepped, and that they would be pissed off too. Message received, loud and clear.

"I wanted her to stop *resisting*." I explained, "I was trying to show her that her fear was unfounded. I didn't want her to miss an opportunity to celebrate that she is, in fact, alive. She made it through."

"But you took away her choice," Elyse interjected. "If you want her to go, fine—make it known that you object. Explain to her, over and over again why you feel she isn't acting in her best interests. But don't force her hand. Especially when you two barely know one another. She had very solid reasons for being anxious to attend. You should have respected that."

"How did you two leave things?" Henry asked. "I'm assuming based on her absence today that things aren't well."

"She doesn't want to see me anymore." My throat closed, and a ball of emotion threatened to choke the life right out of me. "I messed up. I just wanted something good for her. I'd hoped that if she went to New York, saw Jones and the other guys from her unit, she'd realize even if it was in the smallest way, that what happened was unpreventable, not her fault, and that she had an entire unit *who experienced the same things she did* that she could lean on."

The whole group debated my actions. I wished I'd have kept my damn mouth shut. I didn't think I could have felt any worse than I had before the meeting started. Boy, was I wrong.

"You been moping around here like a fifteen year old girl who ain't got a date to the prom." Finn pushed the back of my head as he walked through the kitchen on the way to the front of the house. He looked at me over his shoulder, and apparently didn't like what he saw because he did an about face and pulled up a stool next to me at the prep table.

"What's up?" he asked, taking a knife and the peppers I'd been washing and began slicing.

"You know what's up." Instead of sounding frustrated, too much emotion came on the heels of that statement, making me sound like I was on the verge of tears. "She doesn't want to see me anymore, Finn. She didn't want me."

Either.

It was on the tip of my tongue to say, but I bit down on my tongue to keep it tucked inside. I never thought this would be how our relationship ended. If it was even a relationship. Maybe I'd been so desperate to *be* in a relationship that I'd fooled myself into believing I had one when I didn't.

"Except she did, Stubs." Finn collected all the peppers he'd sliced and dumped them into one of the prep bins. "She did want you. You pushed. You pushed so fucking hard that you pushed her away."

His words stung. No, they *hurt*. Burned even. I opened my mouth to explain, but he pointed his chopping knife right at me, continuing.

"You sure do think pretty poorly of yourself. For someone who everyone thinks has it all together in terms of living life regardless of the one arm and everything, I've never seen anyone think so little of themselves."

"The second the going got tough, she bailed, Finn."

"The going got tough because *you* made it that way. And she bailed because you didn't listen to her when she told you that attending that wedding was too hard for her."

"Isn't being in a relationship all about helping people see when they're making a mistake? Pushing them out of their comfort zone because *you know* that the thing they fear isn't as scary as they're making it out to be?"

Finn set his knife down, wiping his hands on the towel on the table. I tracked him as he got up and poured himself a cup of coffee, taking his sweet time making it the way he liked before coming back and sitting down. Even still he pulled at his beard between sips, watching me instead of saying anything.

"Remember when Gemini left?" he finally asks. "She left that damn Dear John on my kitchen table and just took off. Imagine what would have happened if I hopped a flight to Chicago, stormed her sister's house, forced her to pack up her bags and come back right that instant because *I knew* that I loved her so damn much and that she loved me the same. Do you think me forcing her hand would have made her very accepting of our relationship?"

"Since you didn't even know her area code, I'd think finding her sister's house in a city as big as Chicago may have proven a bit of a challenge for you."

Finn huffed, squinting his eyes at me, letting his coffee cup clank into the bottom of the sink as an exclamation point to his annoyance with me.

"Point being, she came back on her own. She had to work through her own shit. I missed her something fierce, and thought about her twenty-four seven, but I knew I couldn't force her to come to a decision. That's what you did to Amelia. You're trying to force her to snap her fingers and suddenly see things as you do. She's got a lot of things that need healing, Emmett—not just that leg, or in her mind, but also in her heart. She's seen more loss than any of us could probably tolerate. She saw it up close and personal, Emmett. That's gotta do some bad shit to your insides. If anyone needs some grace and some space, it's her."

Grace and space. Even Finn was starting to sound like Henry. I could practically see that written up on a whiteboard at the next meeting after the holidays.

"Just like you need to give yourself some grace my friend. You are worthy of being loved, regardless of who it is you fall for. But Amelia and you, you fit. Give her some space. Let her work some stuff out. Don't be pushy. And for god sakes, stop trying to force her to go to that wedding."

He tapped on the top of the table as an end to the conversation. He grabbed a clipboard hanging over the sink, I assumed, to go do inventory in the bar. Even after I only had the sound of the swinging door to keep me company, thoughts of Amelia still teased me.

I needed to find a way to make it right.

CHAPTER TWENTY-TWO

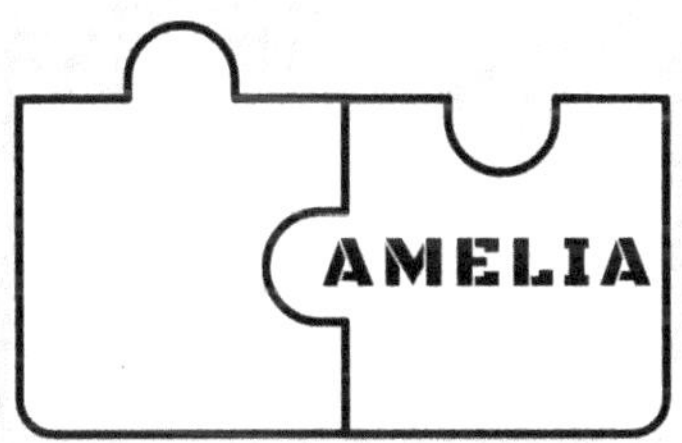

I gave myself a fantastic present for Christmas. I traded in my little two door Hyundai for a Jeep Cherokee. The zippy SUV was high enough off the ground that I didn't struggle getting in and out as much as I had with my two-door. The overall comfort factor of my new Jeep made even my three-hour commute to the V.A. enjoyable—as much as a trip to the V.A. could be, anyway. Gemini also had one amazing Christmas based on the pictures of the newest piece of jewelry she sported on her ring finger. Finn popped the question Christmas morning.

> Emmett: Thank you for the gift.

I FORGOT that prior to the big break up I'd asked Pam if she knew anyone that had suggestions for making a kitchen accessible. After a few phone calls she'd directed me to a website that had all kinds of kitchen equipment for people with a single arm. Everything from vegetable peelers and jar openers, to chopping block stabilizers that held items in place while one would slice them. While I certainly wasn't swimming in money, I got him a few things I knew he would be able to use, like a standard sized electric can opener and a one-handed jar opener.

> Me: You too, Emmett. Hopefully they are up to your discerning chef standards, and you will find good use for them.

> Emmett: Anything from you will be used and appreciated. I hope you find your peace, angel. Merry Christmas.

I NEARLY TYPED I miss you. Twice. Based on the ellipses coming from Emmett's phone, he considered and reconsidered a response, though no more ever came. Emmett's Christmas message hurt my heart more than I thought it would. I didn't know what to say back. Honestly, I was still trying to process all the feelings I had for him.

I'd taken to sleeping on the couch in the living room. After one too many night terrors, Abby said I scared her, and asked to share a room with Annie again. Given Annie still fought for her independence, the couch just seemed like it made the most sense.

Once in the middle of the night, my mom came out to lay with me to try to calm me enough to fall back to sleep. In the midst of my fear, I'd reached out to her and called her Emmett. She took that as a sign that my soul was restless and in search of its matching pair. Her and all of my aunties said endless novenas for me and had the whole church lighting candles for me. Finding my way to being normal was going to take more than a novena, that was for sure.

I HATED FLYING. Not because I was afraid. Or I didn't like the sensation of floating, feared crashing, or any of the other million reasons people hated to be on airplanes. I actually joined the Army because I had a sense of wanderlust that I thought would be satisfied by touring the globe with Uncle Sam. Of course, those plans got cut short. No, I hated flying because those sardine cans they called seats made even a ninety-minute flight practically intolerable.

"If you show them your military card," Gemini whispered, "they will give you special accommodation."

I didn't need —that moment the thought of Emmett

surfaced. His stupid sexy eyebrow cocked up in challenge, calling "check." I did need accommodation. There wasn't any shame in asking for it.

"Will you come up with me?" I asked her, feeling small and ashamed. "It may sound silly, but I'm not sure what I'm asking for."

Gemini jumped into action, marching straight up to the ticket counter.

"Hi, Tiffany." She smiled at the agent, reading her name badge. "My friend here is an Army veteran. She lost her leg in Afghanistan and hasn't flown in an airplane since her amputation. She's incredibly worried that the ever-shrinking space between rows is going to be a hindrance on her ability to move about the cabin, and also may be a challenge to how comfortable she is while in flight. Is there any possibility you can put her in one of the exit rows perhaps? They have more leg room than the rest of us will have."

Tiffany glanced my way, that standard "I'm glad it's not me" pity in her eyes. "I really wish I could," she began, "the exit rows unfortunately bear the responsibility of assisting everyone off the aircraft in an emergency. If you are unable to perform those duties, I can't have you in those seats."

I turned to go back to my seat, assuming that was the end of the discussion. Gemini grasped my bicep to hold me in place.

"We do, however, have accommodations for military veterans. It looks as though all of our extended leg room seats are full fare tickets, so I'm unable to bump them, but I do have an available seat in First Class right at the front of the aircraft. Number 1F."

She smiled and handed me my upgraded ticket, thanking me for my service.

"Fancy ass," Gemini joked. "I'll just be back in 32F

mingling with the hoi polloi while you're up there having caviar and champagne."

Since Emmett forced my hand and I had to attend this wedding, I asked Gemini to join me. She agreed, telling me that she really did want to see her friend, Penn, before he and his fiancé left for Chicago. They were spending their last weekend in New York and truly did have a going away party they'd invited Gemini and Finn to attend. Our flight to New York didn't have any available seats on it, so Finn planned to take a separate flight and meet up with us at the hotel after the wedding.

Taking me dress shopping had actually been a ruse to get me to try on dresses and find one I was comfortable in. Coordinated, of course, by Emmett. As angry with him as I was, and upset at his lack of situational awareness, the ice may have softened just a little bit with the plans he'd conspired behind the scenes.

"Excuse me, ma'am?" A businessman approached Gemini and I where we sat waiting for the flight to board. "I couldn't help but overhear your conversation at the ticket stand."

He shifted nervously in front of us, transferring his bag from one shoulder to the other.

"I fly a lot for business. I'm back and forth a million times a week, so I accrue miles and upgrades like they're monopoly money. Getting to sit in first class really is just a small perk I like to treat myself to as a reward for spending so much time away from my family."

He thrust his ticket toward me with a half-smile. "I'm 1D. I want your friend to have it. I'll take 32F."

Gemini and I both just stared at him in shock. Here was this total stranger, randomly approaching the two of us to give us his seat. I'd seen that kind of thing happen in movies, but in real life? And to me? As a kid I only dreamed of ever riding on an airplane. I never imagined riding in first class, and then having someone in possession of a first-class ticket randomly volunteer to give it to me. I had no words.

"This is the nicest thing anyone has ever done for me." I smiled, accepting the ticket.

I paused for a moment, tracing the outline of the paper ticket. It bore his name on it, Lucas Brown. "I'm Amelia," I extended my hand in greeting. "Thank you for this. Truly."

"The pleasure is mine, Amelia. Thank you for your service and your sacrifice."

He and Gemini approached the ticket counter again so they could switch their tickets. A first class flight. Me. I also internally high fived myself for *accepting not rejecting.* Recognizing that a few weeks ago the old me would have simply suffered in 32E, forcing my body to deal with the situation regardless of discomfort.

St. Augustine's Chapel couldn't have been more beautiful if you'd plucked it from an architectural book on medieval structures. It still bore all of its decorations from the Christmas holiday throughout the church. A sign that stated "We're all family, sit wherever you like!" met us at the entrance.

"That sign is so Jones." I laughed, grabbing a program so I'd have something to do with my hands. "He always wanted everyone to feel welcome. Regardless of rank or station. We were all brothers *and sisters* in arms."

I felt the tell-tale light headedness that I'd identified as the beginning of a flashback, and once again depended upon my secret talisman to get me through. Imagining him felt wrong when I'd told him we shouldn't stay together. But it was the only thing that kept me grounded.

"You're going to be okay." Gemini grabbed my hand, the chill of her fingers pulling me back to the here and now. "Just take a couple deep breaths. We can sit back here if you want." She pointed to the last row of pews. It was then that I noticed they were too narrow. It was an old church, really old. I thought I saw a placard on the front door that dated it back to the eighteen hundreds.

"Oh no."

I whispered it to myself more than to her, but she was close enough she heard my distress.

"It's okay. It's fine. We'll just ask for a chair. No big deal."

Her palm stayed firmly in mine. I focused on her cold fingers, while I searched for an alternate place to sit. I'd been so absorbed with the task of finding a chair, I didn't realize anyone approached us.

"You came! You're really here!" Jones pulled me into a fierce hug. "I hoped you would stick to your word but honestly half expected you to stay home. Not that I wouldn't have understood but god, Sanchez—Amelia—I'm so grateful that you came. Here, we have a place for you to sit up here."

We followed him to a set of pews just beyond the altar. The place where family sat. People of importance. The whole unit, dressed in their Class A's, some with women seated beside them, filled the first two pews. I braced myself for the looks on their faces. Squeezed the feeling out of Gemini's hand, I was sure, steeling myself for what I would see. Judgment, anger, upset—I couldn't bear to look at any of them.

"Sanchez?" They asked one at a time, standing to embrace me. The varied expressions of surprise and delight were not at all what I'd prepared to hear. But each of them hugged me and welcomed me "home."

CHAPTER TWENTY-THREE

I figured since Amelia already decided she no longer wanted to see me, I had nothing to lose. Either she'd tell me to leave, and I would do as she asked, or she'd be excited I came. I chose to remain optimistic. Though Gemini and Finn were both at the ready in case it didn't.

Seeing Amelia in her shimmery green dress, with her hair styled in a fancy up-do, stole every last molecule of oxygen from my body. I wanted to run to her. To shower her in compliments and cradle her against my chest. Watching Amelia have a very animated conversation with a group of men dressed in formal military attire, smiling and carrying on, overwhelmed me with pride and unabashed joy. They must have been the guys from the 10th. Just as I suspected, she'd been welcomed back into their fold with open arms.

"I'm just going to hang out, right here." He shook his head, while he pulled at his beard, disapproval emanating from the set of his shoulders to the pout of his lips. "I still think this is a really bad idea. You're ambushing her in the middle of her friend's wedding."

Finn was the least enthused participant in our group. He sat on the side of "you're pushing her too hard, too fast" camp. Unlike Gemini, who fell headfirst into the "happily ever after at the end of the fairytale" camp.

"I'm fighting for our relationship by showing her I'll go to the ends of the earth to keep her safe and happy."

"If you say so." He shook his head again. "This screams toxic stalker podcast material to me."

I sent up a prayer into the universe. Whether it was for Amelia to not be furious, Finn not to be right, or patience in dealing with my hot headed, and not so romantic best friend—I didn't know. My gut told me Amelia's unit would want her here, and now they were all laughing around a table as if time hadn't passed. She even sat with her legs crossed, unabashedly displaying her prosthetic.

"Trust me, Finn. It's gonna be okay."

I steeled myself with a deep breath before opening the door to the reception. Just as I walked into the hall, the band started playing "Have Yourself a Merry Little Christmas." It was a sign. I was meant to be here.

"Can I have this dance?" I asked, extending my hand just into her periphery.

All of the soldiers at the table looked up and in my direction, confusion on their faces. In that brief millisecond of time, I could tell they were getting ready to rally around her and protect her from someone unknown. Even if Amelia wasn't aware, I knew. These were her brothers. They'd never abandoned her. Gemini looked up first, grinning a ridiculous toothy smile that crinkled her eyes and bunched her cheeks up.

"Gentleman, this is Emmett, Amelia's boyfriend." She pointed at me, turning toward the soldiers who all stood up almost in concert to shake my hand.

"I'd hate to miss our song, Amelia." I wiggled my fingers at her. "And there's nowhere I'd love to be than in your arms spinning around that dance floor."

I half expected her to say no for any number of reasons. But instead, without any argument at all, she allowed me to lead her to the dance floor where she wrapped her arms around me, and smiled.

"I miss you," I told her. "I miss you, and I'm sorry."

The second she put her arms around me the whole world narrowed. Everyone else in the room disappeared, and it was us and the band. Her fancy eye makeup played up the intricate colors of her chocolate-colored eyes.

"My intent in having you come here was honorable, I promise. I knew, in my gut, that if I could just *get* you here, you would see that you'd been building a narrative in your head that didn't exist. I shouldn't have pushed. You were right when you said I have no idea what you went through. But, I want to. I want to be the one you come to when you're scared, or unsure. The one who cheers for you when you have some incredible breakthrough, and who holds you and comforts you when you do your best but still feel defeated."

She hadn't pulled away. We still remained in our little

bubble, rocking to the music which had since changed to another song. Thankfully, still a slow song.

"I've been doing a lot of thinking, Amelia. So much thinking. I realized how badly I need you in my life. I want you in my life. You were right when you said that I adapt. When I lost my arm, it was all I could do. Roll with the punches. Figure it out. Move on. It's what hill folk do. We're expected to just pick up the next day and get back on that hamster wheel.

"As I got older I continued to adapt, but in a way that allowed me to shrink. To hide myself within the blanket of normalcy so that people wouldn't realize I'm disabled. But I never felt small around you. I never felt like I had to shrink. I felt seen in the most basic way. You see me as a man capable of loving a woman. And now that I've had a taste of what it's like, I don't want to get back on that hamster wheel again."

"Oh, Emmett." She whispered, "I'm still really unhappy with you and the need to throw me out of my comfort zone. But today, this whole trip has been incredible. So while I reserve the right to have a very pointed discussion later about how not to challenge someone's comfort zone, right now I'm just so glad to see you."

"These last two weeks have been torture for me." I kissed her with abandon, not caring who saw it, and fully ignoring the hoots and hollers coming from the table.

"It's been an interesting two weeks." She giggled, gently pushing at my chest so she could look up at me. "Lots of talk therapy with my team. I've learned a lot about myself. Both my body and how it is healing, and also a lot about my emotions."

"Oh yeah?" I asked, charmed by her smile and practically giddy that I was dancing with her, at her friend's wedding after all that had happened. "What did you learn?"

"My body is healing. My nerves are building new bridges to communicate, which means that even though it may be slow going, my body continues to adapt to this situation—in a good way."

"Amelia, that's terrific news. I will—" Words spilled from my mouth. If she would have asked me to stand up and do a strip tease at that moment I probably would have.

She placed a finger over my lips. "I also learned that I'm absolutely head over heels for you. And I've really missed you too."

I'd been so taken with how beautiful she looked and how excited she appeared to be to see me, I momentarily forgot the present I had for her.

Nothing else could have been said at that moment, so instead I held her close. We took a lazy spin around the dance floor. Once the song ended, she led me back to where all the men sat.

"In my pocket," I whispered, leaning against her cheek, "is a velvet box. I can't take it out without everyone noticing and since I've got just the one arm, I can't open it proper. If you would take it out for me, I'd appreciate it."

Her face went from confused to delighted. I felt her hand burying into my pocket and withdrawing the burgundy velvet box. My eyes scanned the table to make sure no one was watching us too intently. The last thing I wanted was any unnecessary attention, or anyone thinking I was here to propose.

"Back when I first met you, some shit head little kid told us that if you put me and you together, we make one whole person."

She looked up at me with an entertained smile, as she pulled the necklace out and undid the clasp.

"While that little jerk meant it as an insult—"

"He was all of eleven, Emmett." She chuckled, reaching behind her to put it on.

"Regardless, I've been thinking a lot about what he said. How we do make one another better...stronger. Where you need balance, I have two strong legs, so you'll never have to worry about falling. Where I lose touch and things are just beyond my reach, you have open and welcoming arms. I try to hide in the shadows so everyone forgets I'm disabled, whereas you power through any challenge and dare it to call you anything but fully capable. You and me, angel, we're two complementary pieces of a puzzle."

I lift the conjoined puzzle piece charm, running my fingers beneath the chain, amazed at how funny life can be sometimes. Life punches you in the gut and makes you feel like you'll never be whole again. Then when you least expect it, life sucker punches you with a love you didn't see coming. Amelia made me feel fuller than I ever had the audacity to hope.

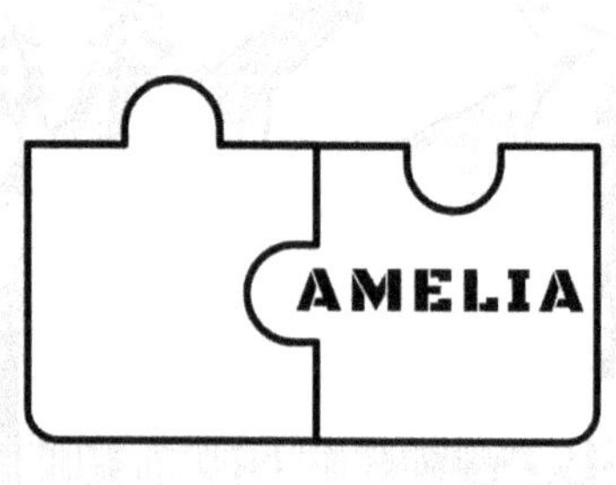

"What's in the box?"

Emmett walked into the bedroom with a gigantic box tucked under his arm. After we returned from New York, he leaned in fully to support my RCC. He joined me at the V.A. and made Pam's day by stopping in and saying hello. She, of course, was charmed by his sexy smile and playful devil-may-care attitude and now they have their own arsenal of jokes and topics they've bonded over. He even invited her to eat dinner at The Tavern and impressed her with his one armed culinary skills.

"Let's call it a belated Christmas present." He placed it on the bed, pushing it towards where I sat folding my laundry.

While I technically didn't live with Emmett, being at his house was so much easier than being with my family in Haven's Cove. Not that I didn't miss them or want to be by them, but the house was small and had too many barriers for me to be comfortable. Most nights, I spent with Emmett. Finn and Gemini offered me the apartment above the tavern. With their impending nuptials, they decided to build a new house right on the lake that was equal parts both of them. The verdict was still out on whether I'd take them up on the offer. They couldn't break ground on their house until springtime anyway.

"Where on earth did you get these?" Inside the box was a very large assortment of vibrators, dildos, feathers, gels, creams, and any other relationship aid you could imagine.

"In our last *Exploring Intimacy as a Couple* class, Dr. Xiao provided a list of suggestions to try. So I went online and bought them and while I was there found a few other things that piqued my interest. I figured why not grab it all and have a whole lot of fun figuring it out."

Emmett enthusiastically explored any and all ways my care team suggested we try to help both of us grow, together and as individuals. At the suggestion of Dr. Xiao, he signed us up for her exploring intimacy class. While the homework certainly was the best kind of extra work you could have, the results were still less than ideal.

While the types of triggers I had from stimulus overload had decreased, and we were able to have sex without me blacking out these days, Emmett worried about my ability to finally summit into orgasm territory. It was common with nerve damage, Dr. Xiao assured both of us, and we simply needed to enjoy the journey without the expectation of "arriving at Las Vegas with every road trip."

"I love you," he whispered as he trailed his fingers down my naked body. "You're strong and brave, but also soft and kind. Seeing the respect others have for you, just makes me so proud to be the one you chose."

I spread my legs open, giving him more room to situate himself between them. He kissed every inch of my calf, working his way to both of my thighs, working the muscle just above where I'd removed the prosthetic. While my body tried to figure out its new normal, we'd discovered some interesting quirks. Like how hypersensitive the muscles and skin were just above the amputation site. But sensitive in the most pleasurable way.

Dr. Xiao suggested trying a Hitachi wand on my pubis bone and not directly on my clitoris to disburse the vibrations throughout the full clitoral region. That was what I tried to focus on while Emmett manipulated the achy muscle of my quad. He held me open with his hand, squeezing delicious pressure on that aching muscle while his tongue teased along the seam of my pussy. He took his sweet time with his explorations before finally diving in and greeting my nub with a long kiss.

It took barely seconds before pleasure and sensation lapped at my psyche carrying me out to where I could lay awash in sensation. With each swipe of his tongue, or press of the wand, or squeeze of that sensitive muscle, I wound tighter, climbed higher. I tried not to focus on where I wanted to go but rather stay in the moment. I thought about how sweet and patient Emmett was. How enthusiastically he encouraged me every time my doctors suggested I try something new. The way he smiled at me across the restaurant when he spotted me staring at him while he cooked. I thought about how even in the beginning just the thought of him could keep my panic at bay. He was my calm. He was my peace. And I loved him.

"Emmett, I think I'm going to..."

Words escaped me as I fell. He entered me just as I came back down, smiling down at me, kissing me softly. The wand turned off and pushed to the side of the bed, there was no sound but our breathing and the quiet sounds of an afternoon in the woods.

"I love you, Emmett."

"And I, you, Amelia.

Coming home may have looked differently for a dust-off like me. While the road was long, and filled me with pain, I found in Emmett someone I could lean on any time I was off balance. He was everything I needed and didn't know I'd been waiting for. While the journey home wasn't a direct path into the waiting arms of the ones I loved, I made it there eventually.

For those who have read me before, you know that I use my mea culpa to admit/acknowledge/accept all of the shit that I took serious creative license on in my book. As a reminder this is a literal last minute brain dump thrown into the back of the book just before I hit publish—so there's probably going to be typos. No one sees this but me.

Incidentally I finished this book on Veterans Day, which felt like kismet and I love that I gave Amelia and Emmett their happily ever after on a day meant to honor all the men and women in uniform. Thank you to every single person who has donned that uniform for the love of their country and to honor what being a citizen of that country means to them. Thank you seems such a small gesture, but I have a wealth of gratitude for all of you.

Thank you as always to everyone who continues to spend their pennies on my stories and my worlds.

I want to say that Emmett has always held a special place in my heart. He deserved to have a happy ending of his own and I wanted to give him the best happily ever after I could. I tried to do as much research as I could on amputations, nerves, neuropathways, and all that other medical terminology. For the nurses, doctors, military members who may read this book and say Willow, girl, you're tripping. MEA CULPA. Seriously. I mean no disrespect and don't mean to reduce or over simply the complex nature of all of those professions and those dealing with amputations. If there is something seriously egregious that I have included here, please let me know and I will absolutely change it.

I didn't serve in the military, and gratefully have all of my limbs, and I meant to show that people can still have active and healthy love and sex lives even with limitations, and tried to show in a positive light that amputees and those suffering from PTSD, can still have healthy, happy, and fulfilling lives.

I also took a huge assumptive leap that Amelia would still feel tremendous survivors guilt even three years later. There were some comments by early reviewers that they didn't feel this was a believable leap, but IDK — I try putting myself in people's shoes in these situations, and so Amelia is written how I would feel if I were in Amelia's shoes.

I had a question from someone on my ARC team about why Emmett would be eating canned potatoes and why he wouldn't just buy them fresh. The ARC reader wasn't from the U.S. and didn't realize that there were fruits and vegetables that come in cans. Just in case you too are reading this and wondering why they'd eat canned fruits and vegetables there are a few reasons. First, smaller towns (especially ones up in the mountains) run the risk of getting cut off from supply chains during large weather events. This is why people load up on shelf-stable food before big snow storms and ahead of hurricanes.

Also, here in the U.S. food pantries typically ask for shelf-stable donations so that they can last much longer and extend the amount of time that they can keep them in their own warehouses for donations. Given both Emmett and Amelia are "hill poor" and both depended on food banks growing up many of the foods they would have seen in their donation boxes would have been shelf stable food. Obviously with some fresh food interspersed, but much of their donations would be canned fruits and vegetables.

In my head it would make sense then that Emmett would learn how to cook because he'd want to make those donation boxes become as palatable as possible, especially if you're getting the same rice, beans, canned potatoes, etc etc week after week. That was my thinking behind it anyway!

This isn't the last you'll see of Emmett and Amelia, as you know my characters dance in and out of each other's stories so they'll pop up here and there, and of course now I have Finn and Gemini's wedding to plan.

There are a couple characters who bounced in and out of this book that you may be wondering who they are. If you haven't read Beard on Tap that is where Finn, Gemini and Emmett were all introduced.

Jasper Raj is a new character whom you will meet in June, in Whiskey Business. I don't even have a blurb written yet, but it will be a small town, broken hero, curvy heroine, mountain romance set in North Carolina.

Penn Ellis is first introduced in Bed of Roses, which is a first love, second chance romance

I have so many stories planned for 2022 and I truly can't wait for you to meet all these couples!

OKAY on to the Mea Culpas

1. I did not serve in the military. All of my information on Army bases, standard of care, and expectations from the V.A. were based on #SIROTI. I also have no idea where a soldier bleeding out from a missing limb would be airlifted to from FOB Shank in Afghanistan. My guess is she would probably have had to been stabilized in a local military hospital first before heading to Germany. I didn't want to get too mired down in the details and lose sight that this was a romance book. So I apologize for all of the inaccuracies having to do with the Military, Afghanistan, or the standard of care for people with medical discharges.

2. Barren Hill, Mammoth Slope and Haven's Cove are all small mining towns that I have always left intentionally ambiguous. My only exposure to mining towns was during service trips I took with my high school to Neon, KY and Fries, VA so as I'm writing these stories those little towns are what I picture in my head but again they could pretty much be anywhere you choose to picture them. I say this because I have zero clue how much snow those mining areas get and whether or not it would be enough to shut the whole town down for two days. But, I needed a reason for Amelia to stay and given its the holiday season what's more romantic than snow?

3. I specifically wanted to highlight female sexual dysfunction. I feel like the romance industry does a bit of a disservice to women who don't follow the standard norm. Not all of us have a functioning gspot, not everyone has a clitoris that works or is fully functioning, some people have hormonal imbalances that make it difficult to get aroused. And while I can understand that romance is mostly fantasy —sometimes reality also needs to be brought into these books so women

realize they aren't alone and that not everyone has a perfect sexual response.

I can speak from personal experience that the female sexual response is a big fucking mystery to most gynecologists and many will send you to a sexual therapist because they believe that any difficulty a woman has is a mental issue —some kind of hang up that doesn't allow them to disengage and fully enjoy sex. It was only recently (like within the last five or so years) that people actually fully comprehended just how large the clitoris actually was and how interconnected all of those nerves are. And I say this because if you happen to be one of these women who went through hell with IVF experience or have experienced ghost orgasms and doctors have tried to pump you full of this or that hormone to try and get you rebalanced, or have dulled sensitivity due to using dangerous sex toys made in China that weren't regulated, or grew up in an era where female sexual pleasure was not discussed, or was never a concern, or any number of reasons and special instances—you aren't alone and though it takes a lot of research and being your own advocate there are female centric clinics that have have more holistic approaches to these kinds of things. And you're not alone and your concerns are not invalid just because you have a doctor who can't fathom someone actually experiencing dysfunction related to biology and not psychology.

4. Other than riding on the BNSF Metra when I lived in Chicago and commuted into the city- I have zero knowledge of trains and train injuries. From #SIROTI limb loss is apparently a fairly common thing working in rail yards—who knew! But again, when I wrote Emmett in Beard on Tap his rail yard accident was an aside that I never really had to think about because he was a secondary character. Based purely on assumption, I would guess that the rail yard would try to settle Emmett's injury with the least amount of liability as possible.

Given that Finn and Emmett in Beard on Tap had a general distrust of outsiders, I figure the reason they didn't trust them is because of Emmett getting hamstrung by the rail yard. It makes sense in my head anyway. :)

5. To the Veteran's Administration— while it's an easy target because they always seem to be in the news for one thing or another that has gone wrong—I'm sure a lot of good gets done within the walls of the V.A. as well and lots of hard working people dedicate their careers to helping Veterans. Any sarcasm or pot shots I take in the book are merely for color and do not mean any disrespect.

I think that is all of my Mea Culpas. I always say this and then suddenly remember something after the fact.

So it's December 1st and I'm about to upload my manuscript. There are a lot of various fun "year end challenges" on Author-gram and BookTok right now and these little challenges had me pausing to take a look back at my year and my goodness. Thank you all for joining me on all of the worlds I've created this year. Looking back at this year I'm just really stunned by all of the writing I did this year and all of the happily ever afters I set free into the universe.

Screwg'd, Bed of Roses, Independence Bae (in the Love on the Air Series)

Beard on Tap and Codename Dustoff (in the Barren Hill series)

Booking Dr. Wrong and Witch Please (Professor Series)

And Thirst Trap (not linked to any others at the moment — but will be, eventually)

Knowing so many of you have joined me through all of these worlds fills me with so much gratitude. Truly. Thank you from the bottom of my heart for spending your days or nights in North Pole, NY; Virginville, PA, Barren Hill, Toronto, Chicago, San Diego, and at Dartmouth in New Hampshire.

As I've said before, writing can be a pretty solitary endeavor, and there are so many people to whom I'm grateful eternally. To my unicorn squad. I love you infinity you bunch of Tuesdays. To Andi Lynne, and the Unicorn Tribe I don't know what I'd do without you. I love you infinity.

I think that's it...I'm sure I'll think of something after I hit publish, haha. Anyhow keep scrolling to see the list of others in this series and keep scrolling past that to see my upcoming books!

You can always sign up for my newsletter to get notifications of all of my releases. Don't worry my newsletter comes out with such infrequency you'll probably forget you signed up for it.

https://mybook.to/WhiskeyBusinessMOTM

Sometimes the best solution for rain clouds, is the sun demanding to be seen.

Jasper

That demanding ray of sunshine had a name. It was Remle Clay. She marched into my life with no preamble and refused to be ignored. No matter how hard I slammed the door, she'd find a window to tap against. The people of Sycamore Mountain gave me a wide berth and I liked it that way. All I wanted was peace and quiet, so how did that curvy red head continue to insinuate herself into my space?

Remle

Jasper Raj. That man was equal parts arrogant and enigmatic. He was a puzzle I couldn't piece together. My career depended on getting his distillery, Lakshmi Bourbon, to join the National Bourbon Association before our big National Bourbon Day celebration. Yet, I'd knock on his door—he'd slam it in my face. I'd send a cookie basket, and I'd watch him toss it to the birds. There had to be a way to get onto his calendar and in my lineup of clients. The harder he pushed me away, the deeper I dug my heels in. When did our little cat and mouse game become fun?

When traumas are uncovered, and feelings unearthed, will these opposites finally give in to their attraction? Whiskey Business is a curvy heroine, broken hero, grumpy/sunshine instalove. Guaranteed safe with no cheating and no cliffhangers! Why not spend some time in Sycamore Mountain.

PAY A VISIT TO WILLOW'S WORLDS!

The Barren Hill Series

Beard on Tap (Finn & Gemini)

Codename: Dustoff (Emmett & Amelia)

Whiskey Business - *A Barren Hill Spinoff* (Jasper & Remle)

Barren Hill Book 3 (No Title Yet)

A Whole New World (*A Whiskey Business Spinoff*, Coming Eventually)

Love on the Air Series

Screwg'd (Bear & Marley)

Bed of Roses (Raven & Penn)

Independence Bae (Bear & Marley, Raven & Penn and some old friends from Dirty Little Secret & Secrets of the Heart)

The Miller Sisters (Love on the Air Spinoff)

Date & Switch (Sera Miller & Bryce Ellis (Penn's Brother)

Rental Clause (Felicity Miller & Klaus Baer)

Under a Starless Sky (Date & Switch Spin Off) – Appeared in Christmas Anthology will release this Christmas

Enemies in Ernest (Acacia & Edwin (Klaus' Cousin)

Salve (Rex Miller & Regina Cole - Felicity & Sera's brother) Coming 2024!

The Murray Brothers

Thirst Trap (Beckett & Lane)

Flirt Like a Champ (Cash Murray & Harlow Prince)

Secret Santa (Priscilla King & Presley Murray)

Harris' Story coming in 2024

The King Siblings

King of the Cul De Sac -*Murray Brothers Spin Off*- (Lennox Shaw & Jesse King) Harlow's Sister & Priscilla's Brother

Secret Santa (Priscilla King & Presley Murray)

The Jones Brothers (Coming Soon!)

Capivate Me (Sterling Cooper Jones)

Titillate Me   (Sullivan Carter Jones)

Extracurricular Academics

Booking Dr. Wrong (Dr. Patrick Ryan & Tabitha Spence)

Witch Please (Dr. Sebastian Doyle & Dr. Imogen Pilar)

Missed Connections (Dr. Phoebe Wagner & Anders Larochette)

The Royals - An Extracurricular Academics Spin Off

Mile High Monarch (A Missed Connections Spin Off)

The Expireship (A Mile High Monarch Spin Off) Coming Soon!

<u>Deck Pic</u> (Sawyer & Wren)

Romantic Suspense

<u>I Will Always Find You & Found</u> (The Jefe Duet)

Contemporary New Adult

<u>Dirty Little Secret</u>

<u>Secrets of the Heart</u>

ABOUT THE AUTHOR